Time to Break Up . . .

"So how are you going to break the bad news to Ernie?" Regina asked.

Amy looked really troubled. "I've been thinking about it for months. I want to do it the most painless way possible."

"Why don't you give him a shot of novocaine first? Oh. Sorry, Amy. That just slipped out. I'll be totally serious. Really. I promise. It might be easier to break up with him over the phone," Regina suggested.

"No. I couldn't do it over the phone," Amy said thoughtfully. "That's too cold."

Regina agreed.

"There's only one right way to do this," Amy said. "I've got to sit down with Ernie, say, 'Listen, I've got something to tell you,' and then break it to him as quickly as possible."

"I think you're totally right," Regina said. "When are you going to do it?"

Amy headed toward the door. "Right now," she said.

Books by R. L. Stine

Broken Date
Curtains
How I Broke Up with Ernie
Phone Calls

The Fear Street *series*

Fear Street
Fear Street Super Chillers
The Fear Street Saga
Fear Street Cheerleaders
99 Fear Street: The House of Evil
The Cataluna Chronicles
Fear Street Sagas
Fear Park
Fear Street Saga Collector's Edition

Available from ARCHWAY Paperbacks

R.L. Stine

How i broke up with Ernie

AN ARCHWAY PAPERBACK
Published by POCKET BOOKS
New York London Toronto Sydney Tokyo Singapore

This book is a work of fiction. Names, characters, places and incidents are products of the author's imagination or are used fictitiously. Any resemblance to actual events or locales or persons, living or dead, is entirely coincidental.

AN ARCHWAY PAPERBACK *Original*

An Archway Paperback published by
POCKET BOOKS, a division of Simon & Schuster
1230 Avenue of the Americas, New York, NY 10020

ISBN: 0-671-69496-0

First Archway Paperback printing April 1990

15 14 13 12 11 10 9 8

AN ARCHWAY PAPERBACK and colophon are registered trademarks of Simon & Schuster Inc.

Cover art by Mike Wimmer

Printed in the U.S.A.

IL: 6+

For Carolyn Marino

Chapter 1

"I've decided to break up with Ernie," Amy Wayne announced.

Regina Green's smile faded. Her face went blank. She shook her head as if trying to unscramble the words she'd just heard.

"What?"

Amy didn't look up. She continued to leaf through the copy of *Seventeen* in front of her on the bed. Her face didn't reveal any emotion at all.

"I said I'm going to break up with Ernie." Real casual.

Regina couldn't hide her surprise. Amy had been going with Ernie Willers for more than a year. They seemed really happy together. At least, Amy had never complained about him before.

Of course, Amy wasn't the type to complain. She was always so cheerful, so enthusiastic, so *up*.

Amy is the most up person I know, Regina thought.

So why was she down on Ernie?

"I don't believe it. I'm totally shocked," Regina said.

Amy didn't reply.

"Totally," Regina repeated.

Amy flipped the pages of the magazine. " 'The Hot New Looks for the Long, Hot Summer,' " she read aloud.

"Oh, Amy, stop being so casual," Regina said, picking up a stuffed pig from Amy's vast menagerie of stuffed pigs and throwing it across the bedroom. It bounced off Amy's shoulder.

"You can't just announce you're going to break up with Ernie the way you'd announce you've decided to get your hair cut short."

"My hair *is* short," Amy said. She reached up and smoothed her straight, blond hair. It was bobbed and cut straight across her forehead, almost a boy's bowl cut. Of course every hair fell perfectly into place, and the haircut, which would've looked absurd on any other girl at Seaview High, looked fabulously cute on her.

Regina picked up another plaid stuffed pig from the night table and began tossing it from hand to hand. "Why do you want to break up with Ernie?"

Amy looked annoyed for a brief moment. She closed the magazine. "I knew you'd ask that."

"Pardon me for being so predictable!" Regina exclaimed sarcastically.

Amy didn't think anything of Regina's sarcasm. She was used to it. In fact, she admired her for it. Amy wished she could be sarcastic too. But whenever she tried, no one realized she was being sarcastic. It just came out cute.

So she never tried.

"Well, if you don't want to talk about it . . ." Regina said, squeezing the stuffed pig until its face went flat. "It's just that I'm totally shocked."

"Me too," Amy said. She was lying on her stomach on the bed, propping her head up with her hands. She was wearing tan Bermuda shorts and a white, sleeveless T-shirt with the number 48 stenciled on the front. That was Ernie's number on the Seaview wrestling team.

"I do want to talk about it," Amy said, finally looking up at Regina. "I need to talk about it. I've never broken up with anyone before."

"Breaking up is hard to do," Regina said wistfully.

Amy scrunched up her face the way she always did when she was struggling to understand something. "What's that supposed to mean?"

"I don't know," Regina admitted, tossing the pig back onto the table. "I'm so totally wiped out by this, I don't know what I'm saying."

"Me either," Amy said quietly. "Totally."

"It's just that you and Ernie are such a cute couple."

"Oh, *please!*" Amy said, rolling her round, blue eyes. "Please don't ever say that again. I'm so sick of being a cute couple."

"Maybe you should make a list of what I shouldn't say," Regina said.

Amy sat up so that she could dramatically toss the magazine to the floor.

"Okay, okay," Regina said. "You're not a cute couple. You never were a cute couple. Actually, you were bizarre."

"Do you really mean that?" Amy asked, sounding really hurt. And vulnerable.

"No. Of course not. I'm just trying to say what you want me to."

"You're making a joke of it," Amy said, shaking her head. "As you always do."

"No. I-I'm just totally shocked. I'm sorry."

Regina stood up and began pacing slowly back and forth in the small bedroom. She caught a glimpse of herself in the mirror over Amy's dresser. Good lord. I look like a stork in this tennis outfit! she told herself.

With her smooth skin, which always seemed to look tanned, her wide olive eyes, her high cheekbones, and black hair braided stylishly to the side in a single plait, Regina was very pretty.

But she never thought of herself as pretty.

She only thought of herself as *tall*. Too tall.

"Hey, Too-Tall!" That's how her dad called her.

It made her furious every time.

What would she do if the nickname was ever picked up by anyone else? "Hey, Too-Tall!"

She quickly looked away from the mirror.

"So why are you breaking up with Ernie? He's such a terrific guy."

"Terrific isn't everything," Amy said bleakly. "In fact, terrific gets kinda boring."

"Well, I guess . . ."

"Terrific is a lot like cute, you know." Amy was sounding more and more glum.

"I only said you were a cute couple. I didn't say you were a terrific couple!" Regina said, trying to get her friend to laugh.

But Amy didn't even smile.

Amy didn't look *up*.

She looked positively *down*.

"I'm sorry." Regina apologized quickly. "That's just the way I deal with things when I'm tense. I make jokes. I can't help it."

"Help it," Amy said flatly.

Regina, her arms crossed in front of her white tennis top, continued to pace.

"What have you got to be tense about anyway?" Amy asked her. "You're not going to break up with Ernie! I am!"

Regina dropped back into the armchair by the window. "I can't argue with sound logic like that," she said. "Okay. You convinced me. I'm not tense."

A loud crash from downstairs made her leap back out of the chair.

Amy didn't move, didn't react at all. "It's just the twins," she said quietly. "My younger brothers are going through their fighting stage."

"How long does the fighting stage last?"

"So far, it's lasted seven years!" Amy said.

She smiled, but the smile faded quickly when she remembered what they were talking about. "You know, I really decided to break up with Ernie months ago."

"But you've been waiting for just the right moment?"

"Yes. I mean—no. I mean, I just couldn't bear to hurt his feelings."

Regina pushed her long black braid behind her shoulder. There was another loud crash downstairs, but this time she didn't jump. "If you care that much about his feelings, maybe you really care for him.''

"Of course I care for him," Amy said indignantly. "But not the way I used to. It's like Ernie and I keep going out together because we can't think of anything else to do.''

"You're that bored, huh?"

"Well—I guess. It's just that a lot of things about him started to annoy me.''

"Like what?"

"Like his hair," Amy said.

Regina couldn't hide her surprise. "What about his hair?"

"It's curly."

"Yeah. It's curly," Regina said. "Go on."

"Well. That started to annoy me," Amy said.

Regina wasn't sure she was hearing right. "Curly hair annoyed you?"

"Doesn't it annoy you too?" Amy asked. "What could be more annoying?"

Regina started to reply, but Amy cut her off.

"I'll tell you what's more annoying—the clicking sound he makes with his tongue.''

"I've never heard it," Regina said quietly.

"Of course you have!" Amy insisted. "He's always clicking. Like a clock or something. It drives me bananas. So does his smile.''

"Now wait a minute, Amy. Ernie has a great smile!" Regina protested. "Ask anybody. It's the friendliest smile in the world. The way his eyes crinkle up when he smiles—''

"That's what I hate!" Amy cried, jumping off the bed. "Why do his eyes have to crinkle up like that? It drives me bananas! And all those freckles!''

"Ernie is a redhead. Lots of redheads have freckles."

"Not that many!" Amy cried. "They're so annoying!"

Regina just stared at her friend. Amy was always the most enthusiastic girl she'd ever known. And now here she was, getting more and more enthusiastic about how annoying Ernie was.

"And his nickname! I absolutely loathe and detest his nickname!" Amy exclaimed, picking up the *Seventeen* so she could toss it down again. "Bear! Bear! Would you go out with a guy everyone calls Bear?"

Regina couldn't help but laugh. "It's a perfect nickname. Ernie looks like a bear!" she said.

"But that's so gross!" Amy said. "It's so *annoying!*"

"You told me once that it was great to go with a guy who was big and cuddly."

"I did not," Amy insisted.

"Yes. I remember. You said it at Sara Dunn's party. The night the couch exploded. You said you felt so safe going with a guy who's big and cuddly."

"Well, that was before I decided to break up with him," Amy told her.

"You changed your mind about big and cuddly?"

"Yes. I have," Amy said decisively. "You know me, Regina. I always go whole hog. There's no halfway with me. If I'm going with someone, I'm totally bananas about him. And when I decide it's time to break up with him—" She stopped.

"Go ahead. I can't wait to hear the rest of this," Regina said. But she was immediately sorry she said it. The pained look on Amy's face told her that this was no time for smugness.

"Poor Ernie," Amy said, shaking her head.

She banged her hand hard against the flowered wallpaper.

"Yeah. Poor Ernie," Regina repeated sympathetically.

"He'll probably take it very hard," Amy said sadly. "I don't want to hurt him. I don't like to hurt people. Especially a terrific guy like Ernie."

"Yeah. Terrific," Regina repeated quietly.

"That's why I've put it off for so long. I don't want to hurt him too badly. I mean, after I break up with him, I still—"

"Oh, no," Regina interrupted. "Don't say it. Please. Don't say you still want him for a friend."

Amy's mouth formed a wide *O* of surprise. "Hey, how'd you know what I was going to say?" Her surprise quickly turned to anger. "You're making fun of me."

"No, I'm not," Regina protested.

Why can't I ever just shut up and listen and go, "Tsk, tsk, there, there?" Regina asked herself.

She walked over and put a consoling arm around Amy's shoulder. She was so much taller than her friend that she had to bend over a little to get to Amy's shoulder.

Amy smiled. Her anger was gone. "Thanks, Reg. I guess I just need a little support so I can go and do this."

"Well, you know you have my support. You have to do what's best for you. But I would like to remind you of a couple of practical matters. Your timing isn't exactly the greatest."

"What do you mean?" Amy pulled her shoulder out from under Regina's arm so that she could face her.

"The spring dance and all of the end-of-the-year parties," Regina said. "If you break up with Ernie now, you won't have a date."

Amy flashed her friend a coy smile. "Oh, I don't know. I might . . ."

It was Regina's turn to be surprised. "What are you grinning about?"

Then she saw *The Starfish,* the Seaview yearbook on Amy's desk. "Hey, you got your yearbook? When did you get it? Mine didn't come yet."

She hurried over to take a look at it. "How bad is my picture? Are my eyes closed? Do I look too tall?"

She started to pick the yearbook up. But then she noticed that it was opened to a particular page.

She scanned the page, stopping at the photo in the upper right-hand corner.

It was Colin Sturbridge's photo.

And over the photo, in bright blue ink, he had written (in very neat handwriting for a boy):

> *Amy—*
> *Love ya,*
> *Colin*

Regina looked up. Amy still had that coy smile on her face.

Suddenly Regina put two and two together and came up with three—Amy, Ernie, and Colin.

"Amy," she said suspiciously, "I know that you want to break up with Ernie because his hair is curly, and he has a bad nickname, and he clicks a lot. But could Colin Sturbridge possibly have anything to do with it?"

"Possibly," Amy said sheepishly.

"Amy, really! That *yuppie!*" Regina exclaimed. "He wears designer gym socks!"

"Yes, he's very well dressed," Amy replied, not getting the point, or perhaps choosing not to get it.

"But—but he's a stiff, Amy! I don't think he bends at the waist!"

"I think he's interesting," Amy said defensively, looking past Regina to the window.

"You think his car is interesting," Regina continued vehemently. "Imagine a sixteen-year-old guy driving around in a Saab Turbo!"

"It's his parents' car. I don't see anything wrong with it. What's wrong with a Saab anyway?"

"It's a yuppie car! Everything about it says upward mobility and crass materialism!" Regina screamed.

"It's just a car," Amy said with a shrug. She shook her head really fast, the way she always did when she was angry, sort of like a dog shaking away a pesky flea, her short hair flowing with her head. "Thanks for the support, Reg. Thanks a lot!"

Regina realized that once again she had gone too far. Why should she give Amy a hard time?

Colin wasn't such a bad guy, after all. And he *was* incredibly handsome. So what if he drove a Saab and had a little polo pony on every item of clothing he owned?

She started to apologize. But the door burst open and the twins came bounding in screaming. "YAAAAAY!" They were blond and light and thin and looked just like seven-year-old versions of Amy. They jumped onto Amy's bed and started using it as a trampoline.

"Out! Get out!" Amy yelled.

"Where's Bear?" Max asked, jumping as high as he could, tumbling into his brother.

"Yeah. Where's Bear?" Michael repeated.

"Get out! He isn't here! Come on, off my bed! You're going to break it!"

"Is Bear coming later?" Max asked, leaping off the bed, landing on his bony white knees on the carpet.

"Where's Bear?" Michael jumped and grinned, revealing two missing front teeth. "Is Bear coming?"

"Maybe later. I don't know," Amy said, giving Regina a meaningful look.

It took a long while, but she finally managed to push them out of her room and close the door behind them.

"They're so cute. They look just like you," Regina said. "I guess they really like Ernie, huh?"

Amy glared at her. "Tell me about it," she said glumly. "He wrestles with them. So they're nuts about him."

I can't picture Colin down on the floor wrestling with them. He might wrinkle his linen trousers. That was what Regina started to say. But this time she censored herself.

"So how are you going to break the bad news to Ernie?" she asked instead.

Amy looked really troubled.

"I've been thinking about it for months. But I

just don't know what to do. I want to do it the most painless way possible.''

"Why don't you give him a shot of novocaine first? Oh, sorry, Amy. It just slipped out. I'll be totally serious. Really. I promise.''

Amy shook her head really hard again.

"It might be easier over the phone," Regina suggested. "That way you won't have to see his face, in case he cries or something."

"No. I couldn't do it over the phone," Amy said thoughtfully. "That's too cold."

"You could call one of those delivery services— you know, the kind that has a guy in a gorilla suit deliver flowers or balloons. You could have a gorilla deliver a note from you. That way, Ernie'd get a laugh at the same time he got the bad news."

Amy put a hand on Regina's arm. Her hand was ice-cold.

"I know you're trying to be serious and helpful, Reg. But having a gorilla tell Ernie that I don't want to go with him anymore is a little tacky, don't you think?"

"Oh. You don't want tacky," Regina said. "Sorry. My mistake."

The two girls sat in thoughtful silence on the bed.

"I know," Regina said finally. "If you don't want tacky, why not do classy? Take him out to dinner at that fancy French restaurant that opened in Marwood Village. You know the one. It's called La Petite something or other. Treat him to a fabulous dinner. Then break up with him."

Amy shook her head. "No good. I just want to break up with him. I don't want to go broke too!"

"Yeah. You're right," Regina quickly agreed.

"Besides, I can't picture Ernie in a fancy French restaurant. He'd probably try to eat the soufflé with his hands."

"Hey!" Amy punched Regina's arm. "Don't make fun of Ernie. Just because he's big and he grins a lot doesn't mean he's dumb."

"I didn't say—"

"I won't let you insult him. I'm still going with him, remember!"

"Yeah, I remember, Amy. I was just making a joke."

"Well, your jokes aren't too helpful. But you have convinced me of one thing," Amy said, brightening just a little.

"What's that?"

"There's only one right way to do this. I've just got to sit down with Ernie and say, 'Listen, I've got something to tell you,' and then break it to him quickly and as nicely as possible. There's no other way to do it."

"I think you're totally right," Regina agreed. "When are you going to do it?"

Amy stood up and walked to the mirror. She picked up the hairbrush and brushed her already perfect hair. She straightened her T-shirt and pulled it down over her Bermuda shorts. Then she headed toward the door.

"Right now," she said.

Chapter 2

"Ernie, I have something to tell you. It isn't easy to say, but it's been on my mind for a long time. No, please don't interrupt me until I'm finished. Just let me say what I have to say, and then you can talk.

"I don't want to hurt you. I think you're a really terrific guy. I've put off saying this because I don't want you to take it the wrong way. But you know, things change. And people change.

"What I'm trying to say is I really think the time has come for us to start seeing other people. Yes, that's right. I don't think we should go out anymore. The year we had together was really great. And I hope we can still be friends.

"And mostly, I hope you won't be too upset about this. I mean, I hope you won't take it personally—"

"Yuck!" Amy stopped at the corner of Dune Road and Main Street. There were no cars coming,

14

but she stood there staring at the Seaview Mall across the street.

Don't take it personally?

I can't say that! Did I say that? I can't say that!

I can't say any of that to Ernie!

She had practiced the speech all the way to the mall, rolling it over and over in her head as she walked. Each time, it sounded more stupid, more impossible.

Don't take it personally.

How was he supposed to take it?

Actually, she had practiced the speech for more than a month. But no matter how many times she went over it, she couldn't think of a way to finish it.

What did that mean?

That she really didn't want to break up with Ernie?

No. She really did.

She was certain that she really wanted to break up with him. Why else would she have practiced the speech for an entire month?

She walked quickly across Dune Road and headed toward the mall. The town had rows of tulips planted along the narrow road, and they were just about to open and bloom. The afternoon sun was high in the sky, but it wasn't warm. The breeze from the ocean nearby still carried a winter chill.

The Seaview Mall wasn't much of a mall by most suburban standards. Sears was the only big store, and there were only about twenty shops and restaurants in all. The movie theater had only four screens. But the town had fought the mall's construction as if it were the end of civilization.

Seaview had always been a quaint little resort

town on the Atlantic, and a lot of people were determined to keep it little and quaint. Despite their efforts to stop it, the mall was eventually built on a small strip of land on the outskirts of the Old Village. Now, a few years later, most people admitted that it was a nice convenience, and it really hadn't changed the character of the town all that much.

It did mean, however, that the teenagers of Seaview had a place to get together other than the beach. Pete's Pizza Heaven, an old-fashioned pizza parlor with a long row of red vinyl booths stretching the length of the store, was the main hangout.

This is where Amy had arranged to meet Ernie after his wrestling team practice. As she pushed open the red- and white-curtained door, she saw that he was already there, sitting in a booth near the center of the crowded restaurant. He was wearing his usual baggy jean cutoffs and a gray sweatshirt with number 48 on the front. He seemed to be reading a can of Coke.

Feeling nervous and kind of fluttery, Amy walked quickly past some kids she knew and up to Ernie's booth.

If I say it real fast, I think I can do it, she told herself, feeling her throat begin to tighten. I'll just blurt it out, and it'll be all over.

"Ernie, I came to tell you that . . . uh . . . we have to stop seeing each other. I don't want to go out with you anymore."

He smiled up at her, his eyes crinkling the way they always did.

He put down the Coke can.

He reached up and pulled the Walkman headphones from his ears. "Did you say something? I just got this new tape. Guess I had it on pretty loud."

She couldn't do it twice.

I'll sit down first, then I'll give my speech.

She slumped into the booth across from him.

"No. I—uh—I just said I was sorry I'm late."

"You're not. Practice let out early. Danny Miller broke his arm."

"What? That's horrible! How did it happen?"

"He was careless."

She waited for him to say more, give a little more of an explanation, but he didn't.

He is so *annoying,* she thought. "He was careless?"

"Yep. That's how it happened."

Did he always have to say "yep" like that?

Didn't he know how *annoying* that was?

"What were you doing, Ernie?"

"When?"

"Before I came in."

"Oh." He smiled again, the smile that used to melt her heart. But now she just found it annoying. "I was reading this Coke can."

"That's what I thought." Amy laughed, a nervous, tight little laugh that sounded more like choking. "Why?"

"Well, I've never read a Coke can before," he said, turning the empty can around in his big, freckled paw. "It's kind of interesting. You know, they don't really tell you what's in Coke. I mean, they list the ingredients, but not really."

"It's a secret," she told him, remembering a magazine article she had read once. "The formula

17

for Coke is one of the best-kept secrets in the world. No one knows it. I think it's locked up in a safe somewhere.''

Why am I talking about Coke? she asked herself. Why aren't I starting the speech I've practiced for so long?

"That's interesting," he said, and made the clicking sound with his tongue.

He picked up the Coke can and read it a little more. He squinted to read the small type, and his freckles seemed to squint too.

Please don't squeeze the can and crumple it in your hand, Amy thought. Please don't do it.

He squeezed the can, flattening it in his big hand.

"I ordered us a pizza," he told her. "The usual."

"I'm not very hungry," Amy said, looking away. Her hands were cold and wet. She suddenly felt dizzy.

You can do it, she told herself. You can tell him. You just have to start.

"Ernie—"

"I'm hungry enough for both of us," he said. "Wrestling makes me hungry."

"Breathing makes you hungry!" she said.

He looked surprised. It wasn't like Amy to make cracks like that.

What's happening to me? I'm starting to sound like Regina, she thought.

"Ernie, I want to talk to you."

This is it. I'm doing it. I'm starting!

He didn't seem to hear her. He was staring past her.

The waitress, a tired-looking young woman wearing a tomato sauce-stained apron, dropped the pizza onto the table.

"Hey, thanks," Ernie said. He reached out, pulled a slice off the tray, and jammed it into his mouth.

Amy shrieked. "Ernie! Don't! It's too hot!"

He smiled, chewing, a string of cheese sliding from between his moving lips. "I like it that way," he said, swallowing.

How annoying, she thought.

"Go ahead. Help yourself," he said, sliding the tray toward her.

"I'm really not hungry. I have something I want to talk to you about."

Here goes.

Can I do it?

Yes!

He was starting his second slice. "You look pretty. Did you change your hair?"

It was one of their standard jokes, the kind of private joke every couple has after they've been going together for a while. He knew she never changed her hairstyle.

He looked surprised when she didn't laugh. She was supposed to laugh whenever he asked her that.

Amy pressed her cold hands together in her lap. "Ernie, I've been meaning to tell you—"

Suddenly a familiar, loud voice interrupted her.

"Hey, Bear!"

"Yo! It's Bear!"

Buddy and Greg, two of Ernie's pals from the wrestling team, piled uninvited into the booth. They were both big like Ernie and both wore gray wrestling team sweatshirts. Buddy was blond and had a pudgy baby face. He had the face of a six-year-old. The rest of him looked like a normal 180-pound teenage hulk. Greg had brown, wavy hair which always looked wet. He always wore a serious expression even though he probably had never had a single serious thought in his life.

"Hey, you ordered for us already! Thanks, Bear!" Buddy said, grabbing a slice off the tray and jamming it into his mouth the way Ernie did.

"Yeah, thanks," Greg repeated, helping himself.

"Save me some," Ernie grumbled. "I've only had three slices."

"Hi, guys," Amy said, rolling her eyes. Maybe they'd get the hint that she didn't want them there.

"Amy. Lookin' good," Buddy said, without glancing up from his pizza.

"How's it goin'?" Greg asked her. "Aren't you gettin' tired of Bear yet?"

The three of them laughed.

Amy forced a weak smile onto her face.

Yes, I am. And if you hadn't barged in, I would've told him so. That's what she wanted to say.

But of course she didn't. She didn't say anything.

"How's Danny doing?" Ernie asked.

"Okay, I guess," Buddy said, taking another slice. "Greg and I took him to the hospital. They were putting a cast on his arm. His parents showed up, so we left."

"How'd he break it?" Amy asked.

"He was careless," Buddy answered.

"There's one slice left. Amy, you want it?" Greg asked.

"No. No, thanks," Amy said.

20

Greg folded the slice and slid most of it into his open mouth.

"Hey, Greg, you ever read a Coke can?" Ernie asked, grinning.

Greg looked back, as serious as ever. "No. But I read a cereal box once."

The three of them laughed as if that were the funniest thing anyone had ever said.

"He wrote a book report on Frosted Flakes!" Buddy added, and they laughed all over again, slapping each other five until a water glass went crashing to the floor.

Amy slumped back against the vinyl seat.

She liked Buddy and Greg. They were nice guys and actually a lot of fun. But why did they have to show up at the very moment she had finally worked up the courage to start breaking up with Ernie?

Now, of course, she'd have to wait.

Maybe she'd put it off for a while. Just a week or so.

No. Stop thinking like that, she told herself. You've got to do it today, when Buddy and Greg leave.

She felt a sudden chill. Her hands were still cold and wet.

I won't feel better until I do it, she thought. Once it's over, I won't have to be this nervous.

"How much money have you got, Bear?" Buddy asked.

Ernie looked at him suspiciously. He clicked his tongue. "Why?"

"I thought maybe you have enough to buy us another pizza!"

More loud laughing.

"No. I've gotta go. I'm supposed to mow the lawn," Ernie said. He gave Buddy a playful shove to get him to move out of the booth.

Greg climbed out so that Amy could slide out. "You're pretty quiet today," he said.

She could feel herself blushing. "I've got a lot on my mind," she said.

"Uh-oh! Look out, Bear! You're in trouble!" Buddy exclaimed.

Everyone laughed. Amy forced herself to laugh too.

"Later," Ernie said.

"Later, man,"

A few seconds later she and Ernie were outside. The sun was lowering itself behind the tall pines across Dune Road. The air from the ocean was chilly.

"You want to walk home?" Amy asked.

"Yep," he said, putting a heavy arm around her shoulder. He kissed her cheek. His lips felt warm and dry. His breath smelled of tomato sauce. "Oh. I almost forgot. I've got to stop at the hardware store and get some oil for the lawn mower. Only take a second." He clicked his tongue.

I'll break up with him on the way home, she thought. It'll be easier to walk and talk. I won't be sitting across from him. I won't have to look into his hurt eyes.

Back in the mall, they walked past the Shoe Barn, past the Popcorn Poppery, past Jules' Jewels. He kept his arm around her shoulder. It must've weighed a ton.

He's so annoying, she thought.

A couple of kids from school waved to them.

They were on their way to Pete's Pizza Heaven. "Hey, you two, why don't you get married?" one of them yelled.

They entered the hardware store at the far end of the mall. Ernie located the shelf with the oils. He spent a long time comparing different cans.

I don't believe it! Amy thought. Now he's reading oil cans!

"It's hard to decide between seven-in-one oil or four-in-one oil," he told her. "Or maybe I should get this all-purpose oil."

He looked at her as if she should have an opinion.

Annoying, she thought. Very annoying.

He bought the all-purpose oil. They walked out of the mall and headed across Dune Road, then down Sandpiper Lane toward his house.

Amy cleared her throat nervously. She felt light-headed again.

This is it, kid, she told herself. No chickening out.

It isn't fair to Ernie, after all. He still thinks I'm nuts about him. He's too nice a guy to deceive like that.

"Ernie—"

"I promised my dad I'd mow both lawns today," he said. "I'll have to hurry. Maybe I'll do the back today and save the front for tomorrow."

"Ernie, I—uh—"

"I don't mind doing both lawns. It's the least I can do. My mom and dad both work such long hours, I don't mind pitching in whenever I can."

"Yeah. I understand."

"Of course, in a year or so, maybe I can turn the

job over to your little brothers. I'd pay 'em, of course. Think they'd like that?"

"What?"

She hadn't been listening. She'd been trying to figure out how to begin breaking up with him.

"Max and Mike. Think they'd like to earn some bread mowing the lawn?"

"Yeah. I guess."

What was he talking about? Why wouldn't he let her talk?

"Listen, Ernie. I want to tell you something. I just—YAAIIII!"

A car horn blared out right behind them. Amy jumped about three feet off the pavement.

"Sorry. I didn't mean to startle you."

She turned and immediately recognized the dented blue Honda. It was Ernie's mother.

"Hi, Mom," Ernie said, giving her a little wave. "I got the oil for the lawn mower." He held up the paper bag.

"Good," she said. "How are you, Amy?"

"Fine."

"Hop in. I'll give you a lift home."

Ernie opened the door and pushed the seat forward so Amy could climb into the back. "You coming?"

Great, Amy thought. That's just great. This'll be real cool. I'll break up with Ernie from the backseat of the car while his mother drives us home!

"No. I—uh—I really feel like walking. I need some exercise."

Was Ernie's mother looking at her strangely? Or was Amy just imagining that?

"Well, okay." Ernie looked a little surprised.

"I'll see you later then." He climbed in beside his mother. He always looked too big to fit into the little car, but somehow he managed it.

"Later?"

"Yeah. I'm coming over for dinner, remember?"

"Oh, yeah. Right," Amy said. Ernie came over for dinner almost every night. He said it was because his parents worked late. But Amy knew he came to her house because the food was better.

And because he's nuts about you, she told herself.

He's nuts about you, and you're going to break up with him.

"Bye, now. Nice to see you, Amy," Ernie's mother said. The little Honda rumbled away.

I'll break up with Ernie after dinner, Amy told herself.

After I do it, will his mother hate me?

Stop thinking about things like that.

She pictured Ernie's mother in the little blue Honda trying to run her down as she crossed the street.

Stop it.

You have to do what's right. You can't keep going with Ernie just because you've been going with Ernie.

That made sense to her. Perfect sense.

She felt a little better. Having come so close to breaking up with him after so many weeks of thinking about it made her feel better.

She crossed Gander's Path and turned onto her street. The Williamses' dog, a frenetic, yapping gray Cockapoo, came shuffling up to sniff her shoes. She bent down and petted it for a few seconds. That seemed to satisfy it. It turned and went waddling back to its yard.

If only people were as easy to deal with, she thought.

I could scratch Ernie's back for a few seconds, then send him on his way.

The thought made her laugh.

"Hey, what's so funny?"

She turned to find that a tan and silver Saab had pulled up beside her.

"Colin!"

"None other." He flashed her a toothy smile. He had dimples in both cheeks when he smiled.

I'm a sucker for dimples, she thought.

He had an adorable cleft in his chin.

What a combination! Amy practically sighed aloud.

"I was hoping to run into you, Amy," Colin said.

"With the car?"

He thought about that for a second, realized it was a joke, and uttered a little choked laugh. "Ha-ha. Very good. No. I just meant run into you."

"That's nice," she replied warmly. "I'm glad you did too."

He seemed excited by the warmth of her reply. His Adam's apple began bobbing up and down violently in his throat.

How cute, Amy thought.

"I wonder if you're available Saturday night," Colin said, leaning out the window of the Saab so he could speak confidentially. She could see the polo pony on his striped rugby shirt. "Rob Litton's parents are going to be out of town, so he's throwing a big party at his house."

His Adam's apple kept bobbing after he finished speaking.

How adorable, Amy thought.

But she said, "Gee, I'm sorry, Colin. I really can't."

His head drooped. The dimples disappeared.

"I'm still—uh—sort of going with Ernie," Amy said, practically swallowing the words.

"What? I couldn't hear you."

"Nothing really," she said. "I can't go to the party with you."

"Bummer," he said. The word didn't sound right coming from him. "It's kind of a shame we haven't had the opportunity to get to know each other better." He flashed another smile, revealing all 146 teeth.

"Yes. Yes, it is," she said, smiling back at him. "I—uh—I feel the same way, Colin."

She realized she had walked up really close to the car. She was leaning down to talk to him. Her face was only an inch away from his.

They gazed at each other meaningfully for a second or two. Then he suddenly looked very embarrassed.

"Be seeing you," he said, giving her a little salute.

How sweet, she thought.

"See you," she echoed.

He dropped the car into gear and pulled off silently and smoothly.

Great car, she thought. She couldn't figure out what Regina's objection to it had been.

She stood and watched the Saab drive off until it

turned the corner. She suddenly felt very angry with herself.

If I had broken up with Ernie, I could've gone out with Colin Saturday night.

She realized for the first time just how serious she was about wanting to go out with Colin. And as she turned to walk up the gravel driveway to her house, she realized she was more determined than ever to break up with Ernie.

"I'll do it tonight!" she said aloud. She knew she could do it now. She didn't even feel nervous about it.

Chapter 3

"Hi, I'm home!"

Amy waved to her mother as she passed by the kitchen. "Dad home yet?"

"Not yet. Dinner's in about twenty minutes."

Amy stopped at the stairway. Something strange was going on. Something was different. She stood at the bottom step for a few moments trying to figure out what it was.

It didn't take her long.

It was the quiet. The house was so quiet.

"Where are the twins?" she called to her mother.

"Gee, I don't know. Up in their room, I guess."

No. Not in their room. It was too quiet for that. They had to be in *her* room.

She found them standing on chairs in front of her dresser mirror. They had taken out her makeup box. They had opened every tube and jar.

Max had covered his forehead in purple lipstick. His cheeks were covered in blue eye shadow. Mike had an enormous black mascara mouth that ran down past his chin. He had bright red dots all over his cheeks.

"Oh no!" Amy shrieked.

They turned around and smiled at her.

They didn't have the decency to be guilty. Or sorry.

"Look at us!" Max said proudly, admiring himself in the mirror.

Amy tried to get furious at them. But they looked too funny. "What do you think you're doing?" she screamed, trying to sound angry.

"Putting on makeup," Michael said.

"Get away! Get away from there!"

"But we're not finished," Max protested.

"What are you supposed to be—monsters from outer space?"

They looked hurt. "No. We're flowers," Michael said.

Amy had to laugh. They were both so sweet. How could she get angry at two boys who wanted to be flowers?

"You look great," she told them, walking up and putting a hand on each's shoulder. "But you know you're not allowed in my makeup."

"We didn't know it was yours," Max said, adding some bold red smears above his eyebrows.

They were so sweet. And such liars!

The front door slammed downstairs.

"Hey! Dad's home!" Both boys dropped their makeup and went tearing out of the room and down the stairs.

"Good lord!" Amy could hear her father's cry of surprise. Then she heard the twins' gleeful laughter.

"Hey, get off me! Get off! Don't get that stuff on my suit! Amy, where are you?"

Amy walked to the head of the stairs. "Yeah, Dad?"

He glared up at her angrily as the two giggling, squealing flowers tried to climb him. "Amy, why did you do this to them?"

That was just like her dad. He always walked in the door and immediately got everything wrong.

"Dad, I didn't!" Amy cried.

He frowned up at her accusingly. "Oh. I suppose they did this to themselves?"

"Yes, we did! Yes, we did!" the twins squealed together. Max rubbed a big blue stain into his dad's trouser leg.

"You always get everything wrong!" Amy cried, suddenly feeling out of control. "You always accuse me of everything!"

She wasn't really angry at her dad. Why was she screaming at him like that?

He looked up at her and gave her a helpless shrug.

"It's true!" Amy shrieked. "Why do I always get blamed?"

Before her father could answer, the door swung open behind him and in bounced Ernie. "What's going on? Am I late for dinner?" His jeans were torn at the knee, but he'd put on a clean sweatshirt.

"Amy's having a fit for some reason," her dad told Ernie.

"Yaaaay! Look at us!" The twins turned their attention from their father and started jumping up on Ernie. They looked like two painted grasshoppers trying to climb a mountain.

"Thanks a lot, Dad," Amy shouted bitterly. Why was she being so emotional? It was because of Ernie, she decided. That's who she was angry at.

Why hadn't he let her break up with him this afternoon? Why was he still here?

I'm definitely doing it after dinner, she told herself.

No way we'll still be going together after tonight.

She looked down at him playing with Michael and Max. They were climbing all over him. He rubbed a finger across Max's purple forehead and then licked his finger. "Delicious!" he said.

The twins laughed and laughed. They thought he was hilarious. His clean sweatshirt was covered with makeup stains.

"We're flowers!" Max told him.

"What kind of flower likes to kiss?" Ernie asked them.

They gave up.

"Tulips. Get it? Two lips?"

They laughed again.

"What a horrible joke," Amy muttered. She walked slowly down the stairs and stood watching them from the entrance to the living room.

"It's almost dinnertime," Amy's mom called. "Boys, wash all that gunk off your faces."

"We don't want to!" they cried in unison. "We want to keep it."

An argument ensued from the living room to the kitchen over whether or not they'd be allowed to keep their makeup on, sleep in it, and wear it to school the next day.

Amy's dad came back into the room, carrying a glass of ginger ale. He had removed his tie and jacket and unbuttoned the two top buttons on his pale blue shirt. He looked tired. Amy noticed that he had begun combing his rust-colored hair forward to try to cover the fact that his hairline was receding.

"Want something to drink, Ernie?" he asked, gesturing with his ginger ale. "How about a beer?"

"No, thanks," Ernie said quickly. "I'm trying to cut down."

They both laughed. It was one of their private jokes. Neither of them drank beer, but they went through this same routine every night.

At one time Amy had found it funny. Now it really annoyed her. Why should Ernie have private jokes with her dad too?

She realized that Ernie had private jokes with every member of her family. What was he trying to prove?

He was trying to prove that he was a member of the family.

That was nice before. But now, it just made Amy feel trapped.

Ernie *wasn't* a member of the family. He was her boyfriend. And boyfriends didn't always stay around.

And Ernie wasn't going to stay around for much longer.

She watched Ernie help her mother carry the food to the table. They were laughing about something he had just said.

How is my family going to take the news after I break up with Ernie? Amy wondered. Are they going to be upset? Are they going to accuse me of sending away a family member?

Are they going to hate me too?

Don't get carried away, she told herself. That's the problem with you, Amy. You always carry things too far. You always exaggerate.

They'll be upset.

But they'll understand.

At least Mom will. Dad never really seems to understand anything.

Of course the twins will be devastated. They're so used to Ernie coming over and playing with them all the time. They just worship him.

She started to get a heavy feeling, like a rock growing rapidly in the pit of her stomach.

The twins'll get over it, she told herself. You don't really get devastated by things when you're seven. Every day is brand-new.

Ernie marched the twins off to the bathroom to wash the makeup off their unhappy faces. They had lost the argument.

Amy took her place at the dining room table. "Smells good, Mom," she said, sniffing the steaming blue soup tureen.

"Of course it's good." Her mother smiled. "It's fresh potato soup. Fresh out of a can!"

Amy gave her a weak smile. "That sounds like one of Ernie's jokes."

"It is," her mother replied, starting to serve the soup. "You look a little troubled tonight, Amy. Everything okay? Are you just upset about your makeup?"

"No. They left me a little," Amy said, trying to sound light, trying to sound normal. "I'm okay."

I guess I should've told Mom that I'm going to break up with Ernie, Amy thought. I should've given her a little warning. She could have prepared Dad. Everyone would be prepared.

But was it really their business?

Wasn't it *her* life?

Did other girls tell their parents before they broke up with their boyfriends?

Of course not.

But most boyfriends weren't part of the family.

Ernie came prancing into the dining room carrying a delighted twin on each shoulder. He slid them down into their seats. The face cleaning had been only partially successful. Bright blotches of blue and purple and red remained on both of them.

"Now we can eat," Amy's dad said, raising his soupspoon to his lips.

The phone rang.

"I'll get it." Amy was halfway to the kitchen by the end of the first ring.

"She might as well get it. It's always for her anyway," she could hear her dad say as she lifted the receiver.

"Hello?"

"Hi, Amy. It's Reg. Did you do it?" Regina was whispering for some reason.

"No," Amy said.

"Who is it?" her father called from the dining room.

"You chickened out?" Regina asked, still whispering.

"No. No, I didn't," Amy said quickly into the receiver. Then she shouted, "It's for me, Dad!"

"Well, what happened? You changed your mind? Tell me."

"No. No, I didn't, Reg."

"Well, tell whoever it is to call later!" her father shouted. "We're eating dinner."

"You didn't but you didn't? I don't get it."

"Listen, Reg, I'll have to call you back, okay?" Then she just couldn't resist. She put her mouth right up against the receiver and said, "Colin asked me out."

"What? What did you say?" Regina wasn't whispering any longer. "Colin asked you out? I don't believe you, Amy. When? What did you say?"

"Later," Amy said. She hung up the receiver and walked quickly back to the dining room, trying to put on a normal face before she made her reappearance.

"Why don't you tell your friends not to call at dinnertime?" her father asked, slurping the last of his soup.

"They don't know if we're eating or not," Amy snapped. "Different people eat at different times, you know."

"Are you okay? You look funny," her mother said.

"Mom, please!"

"It was probably another boyfriend calling," Ernie said, grinning.

Her mom and dad laughed uproariously. They thought that was a truly funny idea.

Amy pretended to laugh too. "No. It was your other girlfriend. I told her to call back later," she said, pleased with herself for thinking of a comeback. Regina would be proud.

This is a conspiracy, she thought. Mom, Dad, and Ernie are in it together.

Then her dad made the conspiracy worse.

"What are you doing this summer, Ernie?" he asked, taking a piece of chicken and passing the platter on to Ernie.

"I don't know. I've got to get a job of some kind. I don't think I want to clean people's pools again. It drove me crazy all summer, going from pool to pool and not ever being able to swim."

"I want to go swimming!" Max cried suddenly.

"Me too!" Michael echoed.

"It'll be warm enough to go to the beach soon," their mother said.

"But I want to go *now!*" Max insisted.

"Well, there just might be a job for you down at my office," Amy's dad told Ernie.

This really is a conspiracy! Amy thought.

"It wouldn't be anything too exciting. We're very backed up with our filing. You could help us get caught up. And you could sit in on the phones sometimes."

"Wow. That would be great," Ernie said, enthusiastically shoveling potatoes into his mouth as he replied. "Thank you, Mr. Wayne." He grinned happily at Amy.

She grinned back. What she was thinking was unprintable.

How could her father do this to her?

Couldn't he have asked her first?

"Amy, you're not eating. Everything all right?"

"Just lay off, Mom!"

"Don't shout at your mother," her dad said, looking more surprised than angry.

Amy apologized quickly. She knew she was snapping at all the wrong people. And she knew she wouldn't stop snapping until she managed to break up with Ernie.

But how can I break up with him now? she asked herself. Dad's practically made him a partner!

The rest of the dinner went smoothly. One of the twins spilled his apple juice, but that wasn't unusual.

After dinner Ernie and Mr. Wayne did the dishes.

Amy went into the den to study. Ernie joined her a few minutes later, plopping down heavily on the couch beside her and throwing his massive arm around her shoulder. He leaned toward her, zeroing in for a kiss.

"Don't paw me," she said, making a face.

"What?" He looked like a hurt five-year-old.

"I want to talk to you," she said, trying to sound hard and cold, and to her surprise, succeeding.

"Kiss first. Talk second," he said, his freckled face looming close to hers once again.

She shoved him, hard. "No. Come on, Ernie. I want to tell you something."

He gave her the hurt look again, shrugged, and slid over a bit.

He looks cute when he's hurt, she thought.

Stop thinking such mean things, she told herself.

The poor guy. He has no idea what I'm about to say. Not a clue. It's going to strike him like a bolt out of the blue.

In a few seconds he's going to look *really* hurt.

"I think I know what's coming," he said suddenly.

Amy practically fell off the couch. "You do?"

"Yeah. I think so," Ernie said slowly, looking down at his big, meaty hands. "It's about Greg and

Buddy, isn't it. I should've told 'em to get lost this afternoon, but I didn't. I'm sorry. I just wasn't thinking, I guess."

Oh, no, she thought.

This isn't happening.

She shook her head. "No, Ernie. It's not about Greg and Buddy."

He squinted at her and scratched his red, curly hair. "Then what is it, Amy?"

"Well, what I want to tell you is—" She took a deep breath.

And the twins came running in.

"Bear!"

"We wanna wrestle, Bear!"

"No, wait!" Amy cried. But she wasn't fast enough.

They leapt onto the couch and grabbed Ernie. Max encircled Ernie's head with both arms in a tight headlock. Mike jumped on his chest.

"Two against one!" Ernie protested helplessly, laughing with real delight at their enthusiastic efforts to pull him off the couch. "But I'll still take you guys—easy!"

Giggling loudly, all three of them tumbled to the den floor and began rolling and wrestling.

"Ow! Got me!" Ernie yelled as Max twisted his big arm behind his back. "But I can break that hold!" He spun around, pulling Max onto his chest. Mike, meanwhile, had a stranglehold around his neck.

Max pulled up Ernie's sweatshirt and began tickling his stomach, a popular wrestling technique with the twins. "Stop! Stop! You know I'm ticklish!" Ernie cried, laughing until tears formed in his eyes, slapping the tile floor with his open palms just like wrestlers on TV.

As Mike continued to work his neck hold, Ernie looked over at Amy, who hadn't moved from the edge of the couch. "Amy, sorry," he called up to her, cringing in laughter as Max picked up his tickling tempo. "What was it you wanted to tell me?"

Amy rolled her eyes and tossed up her hands in a gesture of helplessness and frustration. "Later," she muttered.

It's almost the twins' bedtime, she thought. Let them have their fun. I can wait a few more minutes.

"No, I'm listening. Really," Ernie insisted. Then he did some more floor pounding, flipped Mike over his head into Max, and scrambled to his knees in order to grab them before they could renew their attack.

What an idea, Amy thought. I'll break up with him while he's wrestling the twins. Then I'll probably have to fight all three of them!

The wrestling continued for another ten minutes, growing louder and more athletic and intense as the match progressed. Finally Ernie yelled, "I give! I give!" just as Amy's mom came in to coax the twins to bed.

"Not going!" Michael insisted, red faced and glowing with sweat from his combat exertions.

"Not going unless Ernie tucks us in!" Max added.

Mrs. Wayne looked at Ernie. He grinned back at her. "Sure thing. Let's go guys. Double piggyback time."

They squealed with delight and leapt onto his

broad back, both of them kicking and struggling to stay on. Ernie lumbered out of the den, carrying his squirming passengers.

How annoying, Amy thought, still in the same position on the couch. He's forgotten all about me.

How can he be wrestling and clowning around without a care in the world while I'm going through such torture? It just isn't fair!

It seemed like hours later when he returned to the den, smiling and shaking his head in admiration. "They're tough. Your brothers are tough enough!"

He clicked his tongue a few times. Then he started to sit down on the couch but stopped himself halfway down. "Oh! I almost forgot!"

"Ernie! Please! I—"

He bounded from the room, bumping and almost knocking over an end table in his hurry to get out.

Now what? Amy asked herself. This is it. As soon as he gets back, I'm just going to break it to him. I'm just going to say it. All this waiting and worrying is driving me crazy!

Ernie returned a few seconds later, with a mischievous look on his boyish face. He was carrying something behind his back.

"Ernie, please sit down," Amy began, clasping her hands in her lap. "I want to tell you—"

"I brought you a present," he said, still looking mischievous.

She tried to ignore him, tried to continue. "Ernie, you and I—"

He swung his present around and held it out in front of her.

"What's that?" she asked.

"It's my letter jacket. I know you've wanted it for a long time. I'm giving it to you."

He held it out for her to take, but she didn't move. "But, Ernie—why? I mean—no. I couldn't. It's yours. You earned it."

He smiled down at her. He thought she was overcome by his generosity. "I know you want it. I want you to have it. Here."

"But—but it's yours!"

"I'll still get to see it all the time," he said.

"But, no—you won't. You see—"

"No more arguing. It's yours, Amy. It's a present."

He pulled her up and slid the blue and white satin jacket around her shoulders. It felt big and cozy and warm.

Smiling sweetly, he helped her get her arms in the sleeves. "It's so big!" she exclaimed. "It's—it's—"

"It looks excellent," he said. He turned her around and zipped it up.

"Excellent!"

He stepped back to admire her in it, still smiling sweetly.

"It's—very comfy," she said uncertainly.

He came close and gently put a hand on each of her shoulders.

"Now, what have you been trying to tell me?" he asked.

Chapter 4

Seaview High was a faded, redbrick building built on a grassy hill just two blocks from the ocean. From many second floor classroom windows it was possible to look over the low clumps of trees and see a narrow tan strip of the beach and the dark waves beyond it. When the wind was right, you could hear the rush of the waves, and the smell of thick, salty sea air invaded the classroom.

It wasn't the best location for a school. The nearness of the ocean encouraged daydreaming. The rhythmic sound of the waves had a hypnotic, lulling effect.

Mrs. Marcus's voice was having a hypnotic, lulling effect on Amy in fourth period English composition. She hadn't slept much the night before and had awakened at five-thirty in the morning and couldn't get back to sleep.

From her seat in the third row, she stared out the window, watching two gulls arc through the blue sky over the ocean, then suddenly dive in a graceful swoop.

They probably spotted some garbage, Amy thought.

She turned slowly from the window and stared toward the front of the large and crowded classroom. Mrs. Marcus was droning on about plot development.

She looks a little like a sea gull, Amy thought. Mrs. Marcus was all gray from head to foot, and her nose protruded beaklike beneath her tiny black eyes. Elbows out, holding her open, black notebook in front of her with both hands, she seemed to be flapping her wings.

"And the essential element of good plot development, most writers will tell you, is . . ." Mrs. Marcus's voice rushed on in a whisper, like the waves.

Amy felt herself drifting, drifting away. To stay awake, she decided to send a note across the room to Regina.

Regina was near the door, her feet casually propped up on the empty chair in front of her. She was chewing on a pencil, pretending to give Mrs. Marcus rapt attention. But Amy could tell by the way Regina's eyes didn't move, didn't even blink, that she was far away in daydream land, just like Amy.

She scribbled her note quickly to Regina on a sheet of paper ripped from a steno pad, folded the paper in half, then in half again. She wrote "Regina" on the outside square and handed it under the desk to Cary Foster.

Cary glanced at the name on the folded-up paper,

gave Amy a quick look, shrugged, and passed it to Larry Kerwin. He pretended to toss it away, just to get a rise out of Amy. When he saw that she wasn't amused, he passed it on.

The note reached Regina's outstretched hand just as Mrs. Marcus angrily slammed her notebook shut.

"I have the distinct feeling that no one is listening to me!" she snapped.

"What?" Larry Kerwin asked. Larry was such a clown.

"Regina, hand me that note." Mrs. Marcus dropped her notebook to the desk and stretched out her hand.

"What note, Mrs. Marcus?"

Quick thinking, Regina! Amy thought.

"Okay, don't hand it to me," Mrs. Marcus frowned.

Amy breathed a sigh of relief.

"Read it to the class instead."

Oh, no! She couldn't be serious! Teachers didn't still do that in real life, did they?

"What, Mrs. Marcus?"

"You heard me, Regina. Read the note. Share it with all of us. I see from the bright red color on Amy's cheeks that she's the note writer."

Amy blushed even redder as two dozen grinning faces turned to watch her discomfort and embarrass her even further.

"Come on, Regina. Read the note. No one is going anywhere until you read it."

The bell rang. It was lunch period.

"No one move," Mrs. Marcus yelled. "No lunch until Regina reads the note."

"But—I can't read it," Regina whined. Amy could see the wheels in Regina's brain spinning fast.

"And why not?"

"Well, it's in code. We write to each other in code, see. I have to take it home and decode it."

A lot of kids laughed.

Mrs. Marcus didn't. "Code, huh? Let me see."

"Well, not code exactly." Regina was fumbling the ball. "It's in a foreign language. It's in Lithuanian, I think. Our grandparents were from there, I think. I don't think anyone else here would be interested." She looked up to see if Mrs. Marcus was buying this story.

She wasn't.

"Read the note, Regina!" a couple of kids urged. "We want lunch!" Outside the door, the hallway was filled with the loud voices of kids heading to the lunchroom.

Regina had no choice. She unfolded the paper. She had to read the note.

Amy put her hands over her face. Her face felt hot. Red-hot.

"Dear Regina," Regina read. "I couldn't break up with Ernie last night. Will have to try again today."

Still hiding behind her hands, Amy heard loud gasps of surprise. A few girls cried out. Some boys were laughing.

"Poor Ernie," someone said.

"I don't believe it!" someone else said.

After the initial reaction, the room grew silent.

Amy slowly pulled down her hands.

Everyone was looking at her.

Everyone seemed really surprised.

HOW I BROKE UP WITH ERNIE

So Amy was going to break up with Ernie! This was big news. This was shocking news.

And now in a few minutes, everyone in school would know it.

Everyone except Ernie, that is.

"I hope that was sufficiently embarrassing to serve as a lesson to you all," Mrs. Marcus said, looking up at the clock. "The school year is nearing its end. But in here, we will continue to carry on as if we're the tiniest bit interested in what's being said. Dismissed."

The room erupted in noise. Chairs were scooted loudly back. Books were scooped up, dropped, scooped up again. Voices, laughter, whistles, groans—the usual sounds of freedom.

Sighing, Amy tucked her books into her book bag and hurried over to Regina. "Sorry," Regina said. "I was going to make up a note, but she got me so flustered I couldn't think fast enough."

"It's not your fault," Amy told her. "How come no one's looking at me?"

It was true. Her classmates seemed to be deliberately looking away as they piled out the door.

"They don't want to embarrass you anymore," Regina said.

"That's not it. They can't wait to get out and tell other kids," Amy said, suddenly in a panic. "What am I going to do now?"

"Break up with Ernie, I guess," Regina shrugged.

"What? Now? In the lunchroom?"

"You don't want him to hear it from someone else, do you?"

"No. Of course not," Amy replied quickly.

"Then go." Regina turned her around and pushed her out the door.

"But in the lunchroom? With four hundred other kids around? That's so tacky!" Amy protested.

"Breaking up with someone *should* be tacky," Regina said. She wasn't sure what that meant, but it sounded right.

Amy fought her way through the crowded halls and headed down the stairs to the lunchroom. At the moment she pushed open the double swinging doors, someone dropped a food tray and everyone burst into raucous applause.

At first she thought the applause was for her.

She blushed bright red again before she realized her mistake.

Chill out, she told herself.

No one cares about me and my silly love life. They've all forgotten about the stupid note already.

But as she searched the crowded room for Ernie, she had the distinct feeling that eyes were following her and voices were saying her name.

She spotted him finally by the window. He gave her a little wave and she walked up to his table, feeling her heart beat harder with each step.

He had six hot dogs on his tray, and a plate of baked beans. "Hey, Ernie, didn't you save anything for us?" It was Buddy, yelling from the line.

"I saved this for you!" Ernie yelled. He stood up and threw an empty chocolate milk carton at Buddy.

"Very mature!" somebody yelled.

Amy closed her eyes. The lunchroom seemed noisier and more chaotic than ever before to her. Why was everyone shouting? Why did the plates and silverware make such a clatter? Why was everyone laughing so much?

"I saved you a seat," Ernie said, pointing to his feet which were propped up on the chair across from him.

This is it, Amy told herself. I have no choice. I'm going to tell him now. At least we won't be able to have a big scene, not in front of all these kids.

He pulled his feet off the chair. One of his sneakers was untied, she noticed.

Amy slid into the seat and leaned forward.

Was everyone watching her? Or was she imagining it?

"Ernie, I have something I've been trying to tell you."

"What? Amy, talk louder. I can't hear you."

Four guys at the next table erupted in wild laughter over a joke one of them had told. The laughter was followed by even louder backslapping.

"Ernie, can you hear me now?" She was shouting, but she could barely hear herself in the roar of voices.

Another food tray hit the floor, bringing the sound of shattering dishes. More laughter and applause.

"What is it, Amy?" Ernie shouted, pushing the tip of his fourth hot dog into his mouth.

"Ernie, we can't go out together anymore!" Amy shouted.

He grinned back at her.

"No. Really," she said. "I'm serious."

His expression didn't change. If anything, the grin spread a little wider. His blue eyes crinkled and stared into hers. He didn't blink.

"I—I don't want to hurt you," Amy blurted out. "You're a great guy."

Had it suddenly become much quieter in the lunchroom? Was everyone watching her? The back of her neck felt hot, as if a thousand eyes were burning into it.

She turned quickly and looked around. No. It was just her imagination. No one was watching. She turned back to Ernie.

He didn't say anything. He just grinned.

It forced her to keep talking. "It was a great year. I hope we can still be friends. I really like you a lot. I just don't want to go out with you anymore."

Enough. She had said enough. She had said it all.

So why didn't he react? Why did he just grin back at her like some kind of goofy statue?

Could he hear her? Could he hear what she was saying to him? Was he in shock? Did he need medical attention? Had he died?

"Ernie, are you okay?"

The bell rang. Lunch period was over. They had three minutes to get to their fifth period classes. Chairs scraped loudly as kids got up and stampeded out of the lunchroom, shouting and laughing. The noise was deafening.

"I'm sorry, Ernie," Amy said, feeling the tears welling in her eyes. "I don't want to hurt you—really." This was the hardest thing she had ever had to do in her life. Why couldn't he be a little more helpful?

And why was he still grinning?

"But I can't go out with you anymore." How many times did she have to say it? "Sorry. Please—believe me. Ernie?"

Tears rolled down her cheeks. She jumped up, her heart pounding, and turned away. Her chair toppled over, clattering loudly on the hard floor. She ignored it and started to run out of the lunchroom.

When she reached the door, she turned to look at him. The tables were all empty now. But Ernie hadn't moved. He was still sitting there. He was staring across the table as if she were still sitting there. He was still grinning.

"Ernie?" she called across the room.

He gave her a little wave, just moving the fingers on his right hand.

She turned and ran out of the room.

Chapter 5

"He grinned? What do you mean he grinned?"

"He grinned, Regina. He looked just like a smile button."

Amy was feeling upset and confused, and she wasn't sure she wanted to be having this conversation with Regina. But Regina had insisted that it was her duty as best friend to give Amy a shoulder to cry on.

Unfortunately, Amy wasn't tall enough to reach Regina's shoulder. And she didn't really feel like crying anyway. She had already done quite a lot of crying, in the second floor girls' room after asking to be excused from study hall. She had cried long and hard, immediately wiping each tear off her face so that no one would be able to tell she'd been crying.

Wow. If only the kids who always put her down for being Little Miss Cheerful all the time could see her now. Maybe they'd see that she had a tragic side too.

She cried for nearly the entire study hall, quickly mopping up each tear before it could run down her face. Then she brushed her hair until it positively glowed, squeezed half a bottle of Visine into her reddened eyes, and went back to class.

Why did breaking up with someone have to be so painful?

She felt all cried out, more edgy and confused than sad.

She'd wanted to run right home after school and close herself up in her room. But Regina had intercepted her at her locker and insisted on helping her talk it through.

"Your eyes are blood red," Regina said accusingly. "You've been crying, haven't you."

"I hoped no one could tell," Amy said, trying to bury her face in her locker.

"Oh. You can't tell," Regina said quickly. "You can't tell it at all."

She helped Amy pull on her backpack. Then they headed through the crowded halls toward the exit. When they walked under the big, hand-lettered banner that read, Springtime at Seaview—Tickets $10, Amy felt as if she might start crying again.

That was the big spring dance, and she and Ernie had planned to go to it together. Now she'd probably be staying home, watching TV, or even worse, watching the twins, while the big, romantic evening of the year went on without her.

"Where are we going?" she asked mournfully.

Regina stopped and stared at her. She had never seen Amy so low.

But if she's so unhappy, why isn't her hair messed up? Regina thought. Then she scolded herself for having such unworthy thoughts about her best friend. Regina, stop being so cynical. Even very neat people can be sad.

"I thought we'd go down the hill to the ocean and walk on the dunes," she told Amy. She put a hand on Amy's shoulder and guided her toward the door.

They walked out of the school and started down the hill. A cold, gusting wind blew in off the ocean. Heavy, black clouds drifted in, blotting out the sun, making it even colder.

"Great," Amy muttered. "I'm totally miserable. Now I have to be cold and wet too."

Regina looked insulted. "Do you want to have this heart-to-heart talk or not?" she snapped. They stepped carefully over the dune reeds bent low by the strong winds.

"Yeah. I guess," Amy said gloomily. "I'm sorry, Reg. I'm just not used to feeling this miserable."

"Love is supposed to be painful," Regina said philosophically.

"But I'm not in love. That's the whole point," Amy protested.

"Not being in love is supposed to be painful too," Regina said. "Ohhh!" She slipped and fell, landing hard on the cold, wet sand.

Amy stared at her without moving.

"Amy, at least you could laugh. It's funny when someone else falls down."

"I'll laugh later," Amy said weakly. "I don't feel like it now."

"Then how about helping me up?"

"No. Maybe I'll just join you instead. I'm tired

of walking." Amy plopped down beside Regina, stretched her legs out, and leaned back on her backpack. "Why is that sea gull staring at me?"

Regina searched till she found the sea gull, about twenty yards down the beach. "Maybe it thinks you're a fish."

Amy didn't laugh at that either. "People have been staring at me all afternoon."

"That's just your imagination," Regina assured her.

"No. It's true. In chem lab, everyone stared at me."

"That's because you dropped your test-tube experiment on the floor and yelled, 'Run! Run for your life!' "

Amy frowned. "Everyone was thinking, 'She just broke up with Ernie and now she's flipping out.' "

"Let's not talk about chem lab."

"Do you think I'm flipping out?"

"No. I think you're already totally deranged."

Amy thought about it.

"Amy, that was a joke!"

"Please don't make jokes, Regina. I'm having enough trouble sorting things out." Amy's eyes began to itch. That meant she was about to start bawling again.

"Did Ernie cry too?" Regina asked, shifting the conversation back to what had happened in the lunchroom.

"No. I told you. He just grinned," Amy said, her voice quavering.

"You said you didn't want to go out with him anymore, and he grinned?"

"Yeah. He grinned. His face sort of froze. He didn't blink or anything. He just grinned."

"The poor guy. Was he in shock?"

"I don't know. If he was in shock, would he be grinning like that?"

Regina shrugged and zipped her down jacket higher. "I don't know."

"I don't know either," Amy said, shivering. "I just know he grinned and I feel horrible."

"He must have been heartbroken," Regina said. "Do you think he was heartbroken?"

"I don't know," Amy said irritably. "He was grinning."

"He was heartbroken," Regina said flatly. "He was grinning to cover it up."

"Maybe."

"He had to be. That explains it. He was grinning to cover up his real feelings."

"Maybe."

"And now you're heartbroken too," Regina said, putting an arm around Amy's shoulders.

"No, I'm not," Amy insisted, forcing back the tears. "I'm glad it's over."

"But you're miserable."

Amy didn't say anything for a while. She stared out at the crashing waves. "I'm miserable because I don't like hurting people," she said finally. "I like things to be nice. I don't want Ernie to be unhappy. I don't want to ruin his life. But I'm not miserable because I broke up with Ernie. It was the right thing to do, and I did it."

"Now you're starting to sound like your old self," Regina said brightly.

"That sea gull is still staring at me," Amy said with a shudder.

"Let's go," Regina suggested. She struggled to her feet and then pulled Amy up by the arm. "It's freezing here!"

"If only he had said something—" Amy said, talking mainly to herself. "If only he had choked, or blinked, or barfed up his lunch—anything."

They walked up the hill in silence. The sun peered out from behind the dark clouds, but the air remained cold and wet. The school was deserted, except for a couple of freshmen skateboarding in circles in the teachers' parking lot.

They stopped at the corner. Three guys in a red Mustang slowed down and honked the horn. "Hey, what's happening?" one of them yelled out the window.

"*You're* not!" Regina yelled back.

They laughed and roared off.

"The hard part is going to be telling my mom and dad," Amy moaned.

"You won't have to tell them," Regina assured her. "You won't have to say anything. They'll know."

Amy shook her head. "No. I have to tell them. You know they're crazy about Ernie. It isn't going to be easy."

"They'll get over it," Regina said sharply. "Don't worry about them. Just worry about you. Want me to walk you home?"

"No. Thanks, Reg. And thanks for the heart-to-heart. You were right. It was good to talk to someone."

"I'll call you later," Regina said.

The two girls headed off in different directions. Amy walked slowly. She felt as if she were walking uphill even though the street was straight and level. She wasn't eager to get home. She knew she was in for the longest evening of her life.

How would she be able to face everyone at dinner? How would she be able to keep it together and not let them see how upset she was?

I should be feeling glad that it's over, she told herself. But instead, I feel . . . She wasn't sure how she felt. She just knew it wasn't glad.

When she finally reached home, she walked into the living room, yelled, "I'm home," and ran up to her room, closing the door behind her. She tossed down her backpack and jacket and threw herself facedown on top of her bed, burying her face in her arms.

Time seemed to slip by. She could hear the twins fighting about something downstairs. After a while she heard her father's voice, and realized he had arrived home. "Where's Amy?" she heard her mother ask. Then more fighting by the twins.

More time passed. Someone was knocking on the door. "Amy—dinnertime."

Max poked his head in. "Are you okay?"

She sat up quickly, straightening her hair. "Yeah. Fine."

"Well, Mom says to come down for dinner."

"Okay. I'll be right there." She climbed to her feet.

Max disappeared. She could hear him tumbling down the stairs. He never walked down. He only rolled down.

"This is it," Amy told herself. "You can do it,

kid. Maybe I'll just tell them first thing, and get it over with." She took a deep breath and headed down the stairs and into the dining room.

"Amy, are you feeling okay?" her mother asked.

"Yeah. I'm okay," she said, looking down at the rug. Her hands were ice-cold, and her throat was as dry as a desert. "There's just something I have to tell—"

The doorbell rang.

The twins jumped up from their chairs and raced to the front door.

"Hey! Bear's here! Bear's here!" Amy heard them cry.

She could feel her heart spring up to her throat.

Ernie bounced into the room. "Sorry I'm late," he said, grinning at Amy. Then he turned his grin to Amy's mom. "What's for dinner?"

Chapter
6

"And I had him down for a three-count after fourteen seconds," Ernie was saying.

Ernie?

What was Ernie doing there? Why was he sitting in his usual place at the dinner table, telling his usual wrestling team stories?

Amy stared hard at him, thinking maybe he was a mirage, an optical illusion, maybe if she just squinted hard enough, he'd disappear.

"Wow! I can pin you faster than that!" Michael declared.

"Me too!" Max cried.

"After dinner. I'll show you!" Michael boasted.

Ernie shook his head and waved a hand in protest. He had a mouthful of scalloped potatoes. "Nothing doing," he said finally. "No wrestling after dinner. Amy and I have to study. Didn't you see all those books I brought?"

Study?

He came over to study with her?

But didn't he realize they weren't going to be studying together anymore? Didn't he realize they weren't doing anything together anymore? Didn't he realize anything?

"Amy, are you sure you feel okay?" her mother asked, passing the bowl of string beans to Ernie.

"Yeah. Really, Mom. Why do you keep asking me?"

"You don't look right. You're so pale. And your eyes look funny to me."

"Just tired, I guess." She shot a meaningful look at Ernie. But he was busy making funny faces for the twins. They laughed until they both fell off their chairs.

"Boys. Stop it right now," Amy's mom cried.

"Sorry, Mrs. Wayne. It was my fault," Ernie said. He helped pull the two squirming boys back up to the table. He grinned at Amy. She looked away.

If he grins one more time, I'll punch his lights out, she thought.

How could he still be grinning when she felt so horrible? Didn't he care about her? Didn't he have any feelings at all?

I can't take any more of this, Amy thought. She stood up and pushed her chair back.

"Amy, what's the matter?"

"Nothing, Mom. Just not hungry."

"Well, sit down and keep us company then. It's not like you to be so rude."

What should she do? Make a scene? Run away? Throw the entire roast beef at Ernie?

She sat back down.

"Make a muscle, Bear. Make a muscle!" the twins were chanting.

Ernie grinned and raised his right arm, letting the boys feel his biceps.

"You've really been working out," Amy's dad said admiringly.

"Biggest biceps in the tenth grade," Ernie said proudly.

"That's neat!" Michael exclaimed. "What are biceps?"

Everyone laughed. Everyone except Amy. She glared at Ernie, but he didn't see her.

"Mrs. Wayne, may I have another slice of roast beef?" He took the platter from her. Amy saw that he had brown gravy on his chin.

Gross. How come I never realized how gross he is? I guess I did realize it. That's why I broke up with him.

"Ernie, have you been thinking about my job offer for this summer?" her dad asked, taking a few more slices of roast beef for himself.

"Yeah," Ernie said, pouring more gravy onto his meat. "That was real nice of you, Mr. Wayne. Can I let you know next week?"

Next week?

He was still thinking of going to work for her dad? Even though she had broken up with him?

Amy shuddered as a very unpleasant thought entered her mind. Maybe Ernie hadn't heard her in the lunchroom. Maybe he hadn't heard a word she'd said, and she'd have to break up with him all over again.

No. That was impossible. He'd heard her. It

wasn't that noisy in the lunchroom. And she had shouted. There was no way he hadn't heard.

So what on earth was he doing here?

Ernie grinned at her. He clicked his teeth.

She frowned at him. Then she saw that her mother had caught the frown. Amy looked away.

"Sure. Take as long as you need," her father was saying.

"Couldn't we do a *little* wrestling?" Max pleaded.

"Yeah. A little!" Michael echoed.

"No wrestling until you eat your string beans," Mrs. Wayne said sharply.

"Delicious food," Ernie said, wiping his chin with his napkin.

"Amy, you've hardly eaten a thing," Mrs. Wayne said.

"I—I told you, Mom. I'm not hungry." Amy got up and started to pick up the dinner plates.

"No, leave that," Mrs. Wayne told her. "You and Ernie go study. Your dad and I will clean up."

"No!" Amy insisted, louder than she had intended. Her mother gave her a concerned look. "I mean, I'll help clean up. It's only fair."

"Good! And Bear can wrestle with us!" Michael cried happily.

Ernie laughed. "Give me a break, guys. Not after all I ate tonight!"

"That's right. Give Ernie a break," Mr. Wayne said, pushing himself away from the table. "Ernie and I are going into the den to relax while you clean up."

"He can relax while he wrestles with us," Michael insisted.

Amy picked up Ernie's plate. It was spotless. It looked as if it had been licked clean. He grinned at her and put a hand on her shoulder. She pulled away and quickly carried the plate to the kitchen.

"Why don't you go and relax too, Mom. Let me clean up by myself."

"Now I *know* you're not feeling well. Let me feel your head." She put a hot hand on Amy's forehead. Amy always liked it when she did that. It made her feel like a little girl. It was so soothing.

"Did you and Ernie have a fight or something?"

Amy pulled away from her mother. "Yeah. How'd you know?"

Her mother shrugged. "Guessed."

They looked at each other. Neither knew what to say next.

"You weren't your usual bubbly self," her mother said finally.

"I guess," Amy said.

This discussion wasn't going anywhere.

"It'll work out. Don't worry," her mother said.

"Yeah," Amy replied. She went back to the dining room for more dirty plates.

"Ernie's a great guy," her mother said, when she returned.

"Mom, great isn't always so great!" Amy said angrily. "Lay off, okay?"

Her mother took two steps back. "Okay, okay. I'm sorry. I didn't mean anything." She threw up her hands and left Amy to clean up alone.

Amy took as long as she could in the kitchen. She was trying to decide how she should deal with Ernie. Should she be angry? Should she be furious? Should she yell at him and throw him out of the house? Or should she be patient and understanding? Should she sit down next to him and try to get him to talk about his thoughts and feelings?

Feelings? What feelings?

He had been grinning at her all night like a chimpanzee with a ripe banana!

She turned on the dishwasher, sponged off the counter, tossed the sponge into the sink, and stormed out of the kitchen to the den, ready to do battle.

Ernie was sitting alone on the couch, his social studies text in his lap. His face was red and he was all sweaty from wrestling with the twins. Amy could hear her mom and dad trying unsuccessfully to get the two wild savages to bed upstairs.

"Ernie, what's going on here?" she asked, trying to sound tough. She wished she was Regina. Regina knew how to sound mean when she wanted to. Amy knew she didn't sound tough. She sounded like a cute person pretending to sound tough.

"Hi." He grinned at her.

She glared back at him. How could she have been so crazy about his smile? "Ernie, what are you doing here?"

The grin faded only a little from his face. His eyes stayed crinkled. He held up the textbook. "I'm doing social studies. And waiting for you."

"But, Ernie—"

"I need help. Checks and balances. Separation of powers. It's all just words to me. I thought maybe—"

"But, Ernie—"

"I'll leave early."

"It's already past early."

"Just chapter twenty. Just help me with chapter twenty. We're having a surprise pop quiz on it tomorrow."

She gave him a skeptical look. "If it's a surprise pop quiz, how do you know you're having it?"

"Because we have a surprise pop quiz every day."

She laughed.

"It's no joke!" he said, laughing too.

"Okay," she said, sitting down on the other side of the couch, as far away from him as she could. "Give me the book. I'll ask you questions. Let's see what you know."

He handed her the heavy textbook. He clicked his teeth. She had a momentary urge to drop the textbook on his head. Instead, she opened it to chapter twenty.

She skimmed down the column, looking for a question. "Okay. Here's an easy one. What are the three branches of government, and what does each branch do?"

He slapped the back of the couch, sending up a cloud of dust. "I used to know that!" he said and then smiled at her. "Give me a hint."

"No. No hint. Come on, Ernie, you know this stuff. Why do you like to play dumb?"

He gave her a playful grin and reached for her hand. "I just like to play."

She pulled her hand away.

Regina walked into the den. "Oh!" Her eyes nearly popped out of her head. She stared at Ernie as if he were a two-headed Martian.

"Regina!" Amy cried. She tried to jump up from

the couch, but the heavy textbook on her lap prevented it.

"Are you two back together?" Regina cried.

Ernie grinned up at her.

"No!" Amy shouted.

Ernie slapped the back of the couch again.

Regina blushed and looked very flustered. "Oh— I'm sorry. I didn't. I mean—I didn't mean. Uh, I'll leave if—"

"Sit down, Regina," Amy said impatiently. "I'm helping Ernie with his social studies. You can join us."

"Social studies?"

"That's right," Ernie said. "You're in the third period class, aren't you?"

"I don't take social studies," Regina said snootily. "I'm in the advanced track. So I take women's studies instead."

"Women's studies? What's that? Typing?" Ernie said.

"That's supposed to be a joke," Amy told Regina.

"Ernie, I always knew you were a sexist pig," Regina told him.

He laughed as if that were the funniest thing he'd ever heard.

Mrs. Wayne popped her head into the den. "Oh. Hi, Regina. Ernie would you do me a favor. The boys say they won't go to bed unless you tuck them in."

"No problem," Ernie said, jumping up. He turned back at the doorway to the den. "Hey, don't talk about me while I'm away," he told Amy and Regina.

As soon as he was out, Regina sat down beside Amy on the couch and whispered loudly. "What's he doing here?"

Amy shrugged. "I don't know. I couldn't believe it when he showed up just like normal."

"The poor guy," Regina whispered.

"Poor guy? What are you talking about?"

"He's obviously in shock."

"No way, Regina. He doesn't look like he's in shock, does he? And he ate half a ton of roast beef for dinner. That doesn't sound like he's in shock to me."

"Of course he's in shock," Regina whispered. "It hasn't sunk in yet."

"What?"

"He's going through the motions. His brain won't let him accept what happened."

"Do you really think so?" Amy thought about it. A more skeptical person might have questioned Regina's theory. But it made pretty good sense to Amy.

"He'll wake up tomorrow and it'll all have sunk in," Regina continued.

"It better," Amy groaned. "It's horrible breaking up with someone and then having him sit across from you at the dinner table a few hours later."

"It must be dreadful," Regina said sympathetically. "Hey, I'd better go." She jumped up from the couch just as Ernie returned.

"Those brothers of yours are great," he told Amy. "They're so smart. I taught 'em some new holds tonight, and they picked 'em up right away."

"Good-bye, all," Regina said, zipping up her blue down jacket.

"Hey, don't go on my account," Ernie told her.

"You're going too," Amy said, slamming the textbook shut. "I've got my own homework to do."

"I'll help you with it," Ernie offered.

"What about your surprise pop quiz?"

"Oh, yeah. I forgot." He reluctantly took the textbook from her. "Okay, okay. I can take a hint. I'm going."

He can take a hint?

Amy and Regina looked at each other.

"Shock," Regina mouthed to Amy as Ernie bent down to pick up his other books. "He's in shock."

Maybe he is, Amy thought. Maybe it really hasn't sunk in.

"See you tomorrow," Ernie said, heading toward the front door.

"Shock," Regina mouthed again, pointing to Ernie's head where his brain should have been.

After Ernie and Regina had left, Amy sat alone in the den, feeling a little relieved, thinking about how she had finally broken up with Ernie. She had done the hard part. From now on, it would only get easier—right?

The phone rang.

She picked up the den phone. "Hello? I've got it, Dad. It's for me. Hello? Oh, hi, Colin."

She hadn't recognized his voice. But then she remembered she had never spoken to him on the phone before.

"Amy, maybe this is a bad time," Colin said hesitantly. "I heard that you broke up with Ernie today."

News travels fast, Amy thought.

"And I thought maybe it might cheer you up or

something if we—uh—if you wanted to—uh —go to a movie with me Friday night.''

Yes. That might cheer me up, she thought. That might cheer me up a lot.

"Why, sure, Colin. That's very thoughtful of you,'' she said.

"Yes,'' he replied. Then he couldn't think of anything else to say.

"Well, I'd love to go,'' Amy said, suddenly sounding as bubbly as ever.

"Well. Okay. See you in school.''

She hung up the phone, feeling genuinely excited and pleased. She wouldn't have to sit around and mope for the whole weekend. Colin had asked her out for Friday night.

"It couldn't be better,'' she told herself, smiling for the first time all day. "And maybe this will prove to Ernie once and for all that we've really broken up!''

Chapter
7

Amy smiled into the mirror. "You look good," she told herself. She was wearing a black silky blouse, and a faded denim miniskirt over black tights. She walked over to her dresser and picked up a pair of dangly, blue plastic earrings to add a little color.

"Sophisticated but casual," she told herself. "Sexy but not obvious."

She realized she was nervous. Why else would she be saying such nerdy things to herself?

First dates always made you nervous, even if you were really looking forward to them.

"When's Bear coming?"

The unexpected voice made her jump. "Max, you scared me!"

Max laughed. He liked scaring her. "When's Bear coming?"

"Bear isn't coming," she told him. "You know you're not allowed in my room when I'm getting dressed."

"I'm not in your room. I'm in the hall. Just my head is in your room." Seven-year-olds liked to argue. About anything.

Max stepped into her room. He was wearing bright yellow underpants and an open, red bathrobe. "I want Bear to come," he said, looking very disappointed. "I want to show him my new wrestling outfit."

"Max, you can't wear that. Not tonight."

"But I want to show it to Bear."

"I told you, Bear isn't coming. A new boy is coming. His name is Colin."

"That's a funny name."

"It's not a funny name. Now go put some pants on. You can't run around like that." Why did she sound so shrill? She really didn't mean to.

"Yes, I can," Max insisted.

"No, you can't,"

"Can too! Mom said so."

"She did not!" Amy yelled, getting caught up in the silly argument without meaning to.

The doorbell rang.

Max turned and ran out of the room.

Amy finished putting on the blue earrings. Her hands were shaking.

A few seconds later, she heard her father's voice. "Amy, Colin's here."

"Be right down," she yelled. Where was her hairbrush? It wasn't on the bed where she'd left it.

Her parents had taken the news that she was going out with someone new pretty well. Actually, they hadn't said a word. If they were shocked, or horrified, or pleased, or ecstatic, or heartbroken, or suicidal, they didn't show it.

They had just stood there, blank faced and silent, nodding their heads and looking at each other.

Now, as she frantically searched for her hairbrush, Amy could hear her father and Colin in the hallway downstairs trying to have a conversation.

"Hey—your car," her dad was saying. "Is that one of those new Yugoslavian models?"

Colin uttered a high-pitched giggle. "No. It's a Saab. Actually, it's a Saab Turbo."

There was a long silence, and then Mr. Wayne said, "You get good mileage with it?"

"I guess," was Colin's reply. "My parents usually put the gas in."

Another long silence. And then Amy heard her father say, "I like your shoes. I didn't think teenagers ever wore real shoes anymore. Only Reeboks and Keds."

"I usually wear Nike high-tops," Colin said. "But I like to dress up for a date."

Another awkward silence.

"Do you wrestle?" Max's voice suddenly broke the quiet.

Colin uttered another high-pitched giggle.

That giggle is adorable, Amy thought, finding her hairbrush on the bed after all.

"No, I don't," Colin told Max. "I'd get all messed up."

"So what?" was Max's reply.

"Max, that's not nice," Mr. Wayne said.

"So what?" Max repeated. "Bear always wrestles with us."

Amy brushed her hair as quickly as she could, tossed the brush back onto the bed, took one last look in the mirror, and hurried to the stairs. She had to rescue Colin from those two. Thank God, Mom and Michael aren't home! she thought. Poor Colin wouldn't stand a chance!

"I like your costume," Colin was saying to Max.

"So what?"

"Max, it's very rude to keep saying 'so what,' " Mr. Wayne said, exasperated.

"So what?"

Amy came running down the stairs. Colin looked up, very relieved to see her. He smiled, his 742 teeth flashing brightly. "Hi, Amy." Amy smiled back.

"So what?"

"Stop it, Max," Amy said, still smiling.

"But he won't wrestle."

"He came to see me. He doesn't have to wrestle with you."

"Why not?"

"Some other time," Colin offered.

Amy looked Colin over. He was wearing pleated chinos and a dark green corduroy button-down shirt that matched his eyes perfectly. He had to be the best-looking boy at Seaview.

How nice to be going out with someone who doesn't think that dressing up means putting on a clean sweatshirt, Amy told herself.

"Let's go," she said, taking Colin's arm. It felt so soft and skinny compared to Ernie's.

"It was nice meeting you," Colin said, shaking hands with Amy's father.

Her father gave Colin a weak smile. "Nice car," he said. "Very nice car."

"So what?" Max added.

Colin laughed, a forced laugh. His Adam's apple bobbed up and down when he finished.

He's just adorable, Amy thought. I love the way his eyes don't crinkle when he laughs.

"We won't be too late," she told her dad.

A few seconds later they were out of the house and into the early-evening darkness and frosty air. It was nearly spring, but winter refused to give up. Amy quickly buttoned the oversize cable-knit cardigan she had pulled over her blouse.

As soon as the front door closed behind them, they both burst out laughing.

"Your brother is a tough dude," Colin said, shaking his head.

"He thinks that everyone who comes over has to wrestle with him," Amy said.

Their shoes crunched over the gravel driveway as they headed down to Colin's car.

Suddenly they heard other footsteps crunching on the gravel. A large figure was approaching quickly. The light at the end of the driveway was dim, but it was easy to make out who it was.

"Ernie!" Amy gasped.

"Hiya. What's going down?" Ernie called amiably. He lumbered up to them, grinning. He had grass stains all over the front of his sweatshirt and several small blades of grass caught in his curly hair. "Colin—hey!"

"Ernie, what are you doing here?" Amy shrieked.

"I was mowing lawns, but it got too dark." He wiped sweat off his forehead with the back of his dirty hand. Then he stood there, catching his breath and staring at Colin.

He looks like a big, panting sheepdog, Amy told herself. He's twice as wide as Colin! What did I ever see in him?

"Lookin' good," Ernie said to Colin. "Lookin' good." He stared for a while at Colin's maroon leather shoes. "Hey, I had shoes once."

"Ernie, what are you doing here?" Amy repeated, sounding even more shrill than the first time she asked the question.

But Ernie didn't reply. He was still concentrating on Colin's clothes. "Where ya goin'?" he asked finally.

"To the movies," Colin said. He gave Ernie a smile, but he looked really uncomfortable.

"Great!" Ernie replied, with genuine enthusiasm.

"Colin and I are going to the movies," Amy said slowly and clearly, just in case Ernie didn't understand.

"What movie?" Ernie asked, leaning on the hood of the Saab.

"It's a festival of clay animation shorts," Colin said, his Adam's apple bobbing up and down again.

"You mean cartoons?" Ernie asked, surprised.

"No. A lot of computer-generated animation and stop-action techniques," Colin said. "I'm really into computers and animation."

"Really," Ernie said. "Sounds good."

Amy, looking very annoyed, jerked open the door of the Saab and climbed inside. Colin gave Ernie a little wave and headed over to the driver's side.

Ernie opened the rear door and climbed in.

"Ernie—" Amy started to say. She couldn't believe this was happening.

"I'm into cartoons too," Ernie declared.

Colin climbed behind the wheel and slammed the door, much harder than he had intended. "Sorry," he said, more to the car than to Amy. The car started immediately. The engine hummed quietly.

"I like the old Tom and Jerrys," Ernie said, leaning forward so that his face loomed over the front seatback right next to Amy. "I like it when Tom shoves one of the mice through a meat grinder and he comes out like hamburger. It's so gross. I love it!"

"Clay animation isn't like that," Colin said curtly, edging the Saab smoothly around a corner and picking up speed.

"I know, I know," Ernie said, leaning forward even farther and breathing on Amy. "It's a bunch of raisins dancing around, right?"

"Well . . ." Colin didn't know what to say.

"You're awfully quiet tonight," Ernie said to Amy. He shook his hand through his hair, brushing out some blades of grass.

"I don't believe this," Amy muttered out loud.

What did Ernie think he was doing? Was he really planning on going to the movies with them? Colin would never let him do that. Would he?

Was Ernie trying to be funny? Didn't he realize that she and Colin were having a date? Was he trying to mess things up for her? That wasn't like him.

Was he really in shock?

That wasn't like him either, she decided.

Maybe he just wants a lift into town. Yes, that's it. He'll hop out when we get to town and disappear.

In the line at the Fox Twinplex, Ernie searched

his jeans pockets. "Wow. I didn't bring any money with me," he told Colin. "Do you have enough to buy my ticket? I'll pay you back on Monday."

"Ernie, you can't—"Amy started to say, but the line moved forward, and she had to move with it.

Colin gave her a look, as if to say, "What's with this guy?"

Before she knew it, they were inside the dark lobby. Colin had paid for Ernie's ticket. The aroma of freshly popped popcorn accosted them as they entered the theater. We Use Real Butter, a brown and yellow sign declared.

"Man, I'm starving!" Ernie said, rubbing his belly. He gave Colin a long, pleading look.

"You want me to buy you some popcorn?" Colin asked.

"Hey, thanks," Ernie said. "You've been so terrific. I didn't have the nerve to ask."

Colin bought three tubs of popcorn with real butter.

"I'm sorry about this," Amy whispered in Colin's ear as they started into the auditorium.

"What?" Ernie asked, with a mouthful of popcorn. "I couldn't hear you."

"I like to sit in the middle? Where do you like to sit?" Colin asked Amy.

"Amy and I like to sit real close," Ernie offered, popcorn falling from his mouth as he talked. "Front row. That way nothing comes between you and the screen."

"Listen, Ernie, you can't do this!" Amy shrieked.

"Hey, Bear!" someone yelled from the back of the crowded auditorium.

Ernie spun around. A gigantic, empty soda cup came flying at him. It bounced off his chest and rolled down the aisle. "Greg! Cut it out, Greg!" Ernie yelled, laughing. "Hey, Buddy and Greg are here," he told Amy.

"Go home, Bear!" Greg called.

"Ernie, will you listen to me?" Amy called.

The lights started to dim. "It's starting!" Ernie said. He shoved Amy and Colin down the aisle toward the front row. The row was deserted. No one else wanted to sit that close.

"Best seats in the house," Ernie decreed. He plopped down in the middle of the row.

Amy was beyond anger, beyond disbelief, beyond *beyond*. "Let's just go," she whispered to Colin.

But Colin had already taken his seat and was engrossed in the credits of the first animated short, *Dance of the Raisins*.

Amy sighed and sat down between them. The smiling raisins began to dance across the screen. She slid down real low in the seat and tilted her head back so she could see. She never could understand why Ernie always wanted to sit two inches from the screen.

Ernie quickly finished his tub of popcorn. He began reaching out a big paw and grabbing up handfuls from her tub.

If he puts an arm around me, I'll scream and start a riot, Amy told herself.

How had she let it go on this far? If only she was more like Regina. Regina would've cut Ernie dead with one devastating remark that would've sent him running home in tears. But here Amy was, letting him sit beside her during her first date with Colin, and letting him grab all the popcorn from her tub with his filthy hands.

She looked over at Colin. He seemed to be studying every square inch of the screen.

He can't be that interested in dancing raisins, Amy told herself. He's so bummed out with Ernie being here, he's pretending to be totally fascinated. She sighed again, a sigh of misery and regret. He'll never ask me out again.

She leaned over and whispered in Colin's ear, "Don't worry. We'll get rid of Ernie right after the movie. Okay?"

Colin nodded without taking his eyes off the screen. Amy wasn't sure whether he had heard her or not.

"Hey, Colin—" Ernie whispered loudly, leaning across Amy, "Got any money left? I'm thirsty!"

In the final animated short, a squadron of clay spaceships all crashed into one another and got smooshed into one big, lumpy clay ball. Colin seemed to think it was very funny. He was smiling when the lights went on. But then he saw that Ernie was still there, and his smile disappeared.

"That was great," Ernie said. He began to push his way up the aisle.

"We'll say good-bye to Ernie when we get outside," Amy told Colin. "He'll take the hint if we say it forcefully enough."

"I guess he's just lonely," Colin said, shaking his head.

"Lonely? He's supposed to be lonely!" Amy

exclaimed. "I just broke up with him three days ago!"

They walked slowly up the aisle. Colin looked really troubled.

"I'm sorry if he's ruined our date," Amy said miserably.

"No. Of course he hasn't," Colin said, but he wasn't very convincing.

"I wanted it to go well," Amy said, giving him her warmest, sexiest smile.

"Well, it hasn't been so bad," Colin lied.

"Let me handle Ernie," Amy said, taking Colin's arm. "As soon as he's gone, we can go get something to eat."

Those words, and the way she took his arm, seemed to cheer Colin up a little.

Outside, a cold wind from the ocean swept down the main street of town in a steady gust. People hurried to their cars, bundling sweaters and coats around them.

Ernie trotted over to talk to Buddy and Greg. They started playfully shoving one another around, and Ernie backed into an old lady. A wooden cane went flying from her hand, and she would have toppled over if Ernie hadn't recovered quickly and caught her.

"Let go of me!" she screamed. "Hands off me!"

Ernie was apologizing sincerely as he retrieved her cane and put it back in her hand. Buddy and Greg thought the whole scene was hilarious.

"Let's get out of here while Ernie's busy with his wrestling team pals," Amy said, pulling Colin toward the car.

"We can't," Colin said, shaking his head sadly. "Look."

He was pointing to the car. Amy couldn't figure out where he wanted her to see. "Come on, let's go!" she said impatiently.

"Look," Colin repeated.

Then she saw the flat tire.

"Oh, no. By the time you put on the spare, Ernie will be back."

"Put on the spare?" Colin suddenly grew a lot paler. "I've never—uh—I'll get dirty—uh—" He looked over at Ernie, clowning around with his wrestling pals. "I guess I could give it a try."

He pulled open the trunk and struggled to get the spare out. "This thing is heavier than it looks," he complained.

He's so cute when he whines like that, Amy thought.

Colin dropped the tire onto the sidewalk. Now he was holding two parts of the jack, trying to figure out how they fit together. "There aren't any instructions or anything with this," he complained. "Oh, look, I got a grease stain on my pants." He still hadn't pieced the jack together. "Now, where does this go?" he asked himself. "Under the car, do you think?"

"Uh-oh," Amy said. She saw that Ernie had said good-bye to Buddy and Greg and was heading back to them.

"Thanks for waiting up," Ernie said to Amy.

"We didn't," Amy groaned, rolling her eyes.

"We've got a little problem," Colin said sadly. He pointed to the flat tire.

"No problem at all," Ernie said cheerfully. "I'll do it for you, man. I love changing tires."

"Really? You'll change it for me?" Colin seemed stunned.

"Like I said—no problem."

"Thanks, Ernie. Thanks a lot!" The color returned to Colin's face.

A few seconds later the car was jacked up and Ernie was working away with a lug wrench. Amy stood on the corner, shivering and tapping her foot impatiently, trying to figure out a way to rescue the evening. She decided it was too late.

Colin stood with his arms crossed, admiring Ernie's work and uttering encouragements.

"Really. It isn't that hard," Ernie kept insisting. But Colin called Ernie a mechanical genius and repeated again and again how Ernie was saving his life.

After a few minutes the tire was changed. Ernie tossed the flat tire into the trunk and slammed the trunk. He emerged covered in dirt and thick, black grease.

"Your sweatshirt—it's torn," Colin declared, looking horrified.

"No problem." Ernie grinned. "It was already torn."

"Can we go now?" Amy asked. "Maybe we can drop Ernie off—"

"How can I ever repay you?" Colin asked Ernie. "Are you hungry? Let's go get some pizza. Okay? It's the least I can do."

"Hey, thanks," Ernie said. He gave Amy a big smile and climbed into the backseat.

Amy glared at Colin.

Colin shrugged. "What could I do? He changed the tire."

A lot of kids Amy knew from school were at Pete's Pizza Heaven. None of them seemed to find it strange that she was out with Ernie and Colin.

Amy sat glumly nibbling at the edge of a pizza slice while Colin and Ernie kidded around and wolfed down the rest of the pizza. What a horrible evening. Amy knew that her first date with Colin would also be her last.

And it was all Ernie's fault.

She remained silent as Colin drove her home. What could she say? Colin and Ernie were talking about the Red Sox. Amy stared out the window at the passing dunes, dark and still.

Finally they were pulling up her driveway. The house was dark except for the yellow porch light. She opened the door and stepped out onto the drive.

I wonder if he'll kiss me goodnight. The thought flashed through her mind. Don't be ridiculous, she told herself. He never wants to talk to you again.

Colin came around to her side and walked her to the front door. They stopped and faced each other under the porch light. The wind made the trees shift and whisper. An owl hooted softly nearby.

"Thank you," she said quietly, giving him her best smile.

Colin smiled back at her. "I had a really nice time," he said, staring into her eyes.

"Me too," Ernie said. He had walked up to the porch with them.

Chapter 8

Saturday morning Amy awoke with Ernie's face looming over her. "Stop grinning!" she shouted. The face vanished. She realized she must have been dreaming.

But the night before had been far from a dream.

"I've got to do something about Ernie," she muttered to herself, yawning. "I can't let him get away with this."

A narrow shaft of bright yellow sunlight poured into the room from the crack beneath the lowered window shade. She tried to get up from bed, but discovered to her annoyance that she had slept on her right arm, and now it was tingling all over and refusing to move.

"Ouch." She pulled the limp arm out from under the sheet with her good arm and started swinging it back and forth, trying to get some feeling back into it. "This day is starting out just great," she told herself.

She flopped back onto her pillow and stared glumly up at the ceiling. What was that racket outside?

She could hear the twins laughing and shouting out there. She heard a car door slam. More high-pitched laughing. "They're at it awfully early," she told herself. "Or did I sleep late?"

No. The clock on her dresser said 9:11. Early for a Saturday morning. So what was going on down there?

She slid out of bed without leaning on her still-useless arm, walked over to the window, and lifted the shade.

It took her eyes a short while to adjust to the bright sunlight. She pulled open the window and looked down to the driveway.

There was Ernie, washing her father's car. The twins were on the grass behind him, having a water fight with two large, yellow sponges.

"I don't believe this!" Amy cried.

Ernie looked up at the sound of her voice and gave her one of his all-too-familiar boyish grins. He raised the garden hose in his hand and sent a splash of water up the side of the house almost to Amy's window. The twins thought it was hilarious.

Amy was not amused.

"Ernie," she shouted. "I've got to talk to you."

He cupped his hand behind his ear. He couldn't hear her over the rush of the hose and the twins' raucous laughter.

"I'll be right down," she shouted angrily.

She pulled on a pair of wrinkled tan shorts and a black- and white-striped T-shirt and stormed down the stairs without even brushing her hair. I'm going to get rid of him once and for all. I broke up with him. And he knows it. So why is he the last thing I see at night and the first thing I see in the morning?

She stomped barefoot into the kitchen, heading to the back door.

"Good morning," her mother said brightly. She was stirring pancake batter in a large pink mixing bowl. "It's a beautiful day."

"Is it?" Amy snapped, making it very clear that she didn't agree.

"Sorry. Did you get up on the wrong side of the bed this morning?"

"What's Ernie doing here?" Amy demanded, ignoring her mother's question.

"He came over early to wash the car. Wasn't that nice of him?"

"No."

"Amy, what—good lord! You didn't brush your hair." Her mother looked truly shocked. Amy never came downstairs without making sure her hair was perfect first.

"I broke up with Ernie, mother," Amy said, running a hand through her short, tangled hair. "He isn't supposed to be here."

Her mother looked down into her mixing bowl. "Tell that to the boys," she said, stirring harder.

"I can't let two seven-year-olds run my life!" Amy screamed.

"You don't have to shout, dear."

Amy opened the back door and stepped out onto the drive. The gravel felt warm under her feet. The sky was bright blue for the first time that spring. The sun was already high. It felt like a summer day.

"Ernie, I need to talk to you!" Amy yelled, stepping gingerly over the gravel.

Ernie shut off the hose and put it down. "She needs me, guys," he said cheerfully to the twins.

"Aw, Bear. What about our water fight?"

"Later." He came walking over to her. Both legs of his gray sweatpants were soaked with soapy water. His blue and white Seaview sweatshirt was drenched with sweat. "Morning," he said.

She answered with a frown and pulled him by the hand to the side of the garage. He rested against the shingles. She started to pace back and forth over the grass.

"Ernie, what can I say?"

"What."

"I know you feel bad. I feel bad too. But I meant what I said in the lunchroom. Every word of it."

"Yeah," Ernie said, expressionless, scratching his freckled nose.

"You're a great guy, Ernie. We had a lot of fun together."

"Uh-huh." Still scratching his nose.

"But I really think I'm doing the right thing. The right thing for both of us."

"I'm soaked. Look at me."

"We can't see each other anymore. Okay?"

"Look at my back. The boys turned the hose on me when I wasn't looking."

"I really don't want to see you at all for a while. You understand—don't you?"

Ernie shrugged. He started to walk back toward the driveway.

At least he didn't grin, Amy thought. *I'd* have to turn the hose on him if he grinned.

Ernie walked past the car and continued down the drive. At the bottom of the driveway, he started to jog. Amy watched him until he jogged out of sight.

"Hey, where's Bear going?" Michael demanded.

"He had to leave," Amy told him.

Her father poked his head out from the kitchen window. "Don't worry," he told the boys. "He'll be back."

"He'd better not," Amy muttered to herself.

"Pancakes!" her father yelled cheerfully. "Everyone in for pancakes!"

The beach was bright white, and the low sea cliffs that formed a natural jetty glistened in the sunlight like a string of dark jewels. The waves were still tall and frothy and crashed noisily, close to shore. Clumps of green and black seaweed had been tossed up by the waves and left behind, forming a jagged border that stretched as far as the eye could see.

Regina and Amy spread their blanket several yards behind the sparkling line of seaweed and looked around. A lot of kids from Seaview were there. The first really hot day meant only one thing—get to the beach and start working on your tan!

"I know I *look* pale," Amy said, slapping some tanning lotion on her legs. "But I also *feel* real pale."

"We look like Puffed Rice," Regina agreed.

Amy frowned. "You really have a way with words, Reg. But you look okay. You're lucky. You have dark skin. You always look tanned."

"Now if they only made a bathing suit that took

six inches off your height—" Regina said wistfully She twisted her long, black hair back and tied it with a rubber band. "Hey, isn't that Colin over there?"

"What? Where?" Amy had started to lie down, but she snapped straight up at those words. Colin smiled and waved from several blankets down. "Oh, no," Amy moaned.

"Amy, how can you be so fickle? Last night you were nuts about Colin. Today, you don't want him to wave to you on the beach?"

"Last night was a disaster," Amy wailed. "I'll be embarrassed about it for the rest of my life. Every time I think about last night, I get all itchy and feel like shriveling up and blowing away like a dandelion or something."

"That's funny. I get the same feeling around Colin!" Regina cracked.

"Oh, no. Here he comes. What am I going to do?"

"First, get that look of horror off your face!"

Amy got her smile in place as Colin came up to them. He was looking very sporty in a white alligator T-shirt and Hawaiian baggies. He was carrying a CD boom box on his shoulder.

"Hi, Colin. About last night—" Amy started, her smile fading immediately.

"About last night—" Colin said just a half second after Amy.

"Hi, Colin," Regina interrupted loudly.

"Oh, hi, Regina," Colin said, not looking at her but instead staring at Amy, a silly smile glued to his face. "How ya doin'?"

"I accidentally swallowed a rhinoceros this morning," Regina said.

"That's nice," Colin said, smiling at Amy.

"About last night, I'm really sorry," Colin said.

"No. I'm sorry," Amy insisted.

"No. Really. I'm sorry."

"Colin. Please. I'm sorry."

"I'm sorry too," Regina said. They both turned to look at her. "Just trying to help," she shrugged.

"I never should've let Ernie tag along," Colin said, quickly forgetting Regina's presence again.

"That was my fault. He was my—uh—friend. I should've sent him away."

"It would have been a really fun evening—if Ernie hadn't been there," Colin said.

"That's really nice of you to say," Amy replied, tossing her perfect blond hair, looking a little pleased, a little embarrassed. "I think so too."

"I don't believe it," Regina interrupted, shielding her eyes and looking toward the water. "Some kids are actually going in."

They watched several kids from their class plunging into the tall, cold waves. Over the steady roar of the waves came high-pitched yelps and shrieks, and a lot of enthusiastic laughter. A devilish look spread over Colin's face. "What do you say, Amy? Let's go in too."

He didn't give her a choice. He grabbed her hand and pulled her up from the blanket. Amy didn't really want to go. For one thing, she didn't want to get her new bathing suit wet. For another, she hated cold water. She seldom ventured into the ocean until mid-July at the earliest.

But Colin was trying to be fun and daring, two

things that didn't exactly come naturally to him. And he was obviously doing it to impress her. So Amy decided she'd better go along.

He pulled her toward his blanket to put down his boom box.

"I'll just stay here," Regina called after them, but they were already too far away to hear her.

"We can come back to my blanket after our swim and listen to some CDs," Colin said.

A few seconds later they were at the water's edge, staring at the tumbling, tossing waters, and wondering to themselves if this was such a good idea after all.

"The secret is to dive in and get your whole body wet all at once," Colin said, trying unsuccessfully to hide the fact that he was shivering.

"Yes," Amy said weakly. It didn't seem like much of a reply, but it was all she could think of.

"Here goes," Colin said, preparing to take a running leap.

"Okay," Amy said. Another brilliant reply.

Colin took four long strides, then dived low into a tall, whitecapped wave. He disappeared in the wave for a few seconds. The wave rolled past him and crashed onto the beach. Colin surfaced, stood up, and waved to Amy. "Come on!" he called. "It's not too—" A wave crashed over his head. After it passed, he bobbed back up spluttering.

Amy took a few tentative steps. "Ow! My ankles!"

"You've got to run in," Colin called.

"It's too cold," Amy shouted. "My ankles. It's freezing my ankles!"

"Come on!" Colin urged, splashing and thrashing over a rolling wave.

"I'm going back," Amy told him. "Sorry."

"I'll meet you at the blanket," Colin called. "I'm just going to swim a little bit—since I'm already in."

Amy started walking quickly away from the water. She looked for Regina and finally spotted her walking with a couple of girls toward the stone jetty. Amy talked for a few minutes to some kids from her class and then headed to Colin's blanket.

"Oh, no!" she cried when she got close to it.

Ernie was lying there on his back, holding a copy of *Sport* magazine above his face.

She stood for a few seconds, trying to decide whether to run away or confront him. He finished his paragraph and slowly looked up.

"Ernie, what are you doing here?" she demanded.

"Just catching some rays." He scooted over a bit and slapped at the blanket. "Plenty of room." He started to read his magazine.

"Ernie, we just had another serious talk a couple of hours ago. Remember? By my garage?"

He grunted a reply without looking up from the magazine.

"So what are you doing here?"

"I told you," he said quietly. "Catching some rays."

"But, Ernie—" Amy tried to get the frantic sound out of her voice, but she couldn't. She decided to take a more practical approach. "You shouldn't be out in the sun. You have red hair and fair skin," she said.

"That's why I'm holding the magazine over my face," was Ernie's practical reply. He grinned at her mischievously from under the magazine.

"This is Colin's blanket," Amy said angrily. "I'm here with Colin, and he's going to be very unhappy if—"

What was that commotion in the water?

Some kids were shouting. People were standing and pointing out toward the horizon. The laughter had stopped.

"Look, it's Colin!" Amy cried.

The waves had carried Colin out too far. He was struggling to get back. But he was being carried farther and farther out.

"There's no lifeguard!" Amy realized. It was too early in the season. "Why doesn't somebody do something? He'll drown!"

"I'd better go get him," Ernie said calmly. He leapt to his feet, tossed down the magazine, and went bounding toward the water. A few seconds later he had dived into the waves and was swimming with long strokes in a straight line toward the floundering Colin.

The crowd gasped as Colin's head disappeared under the rolling, dark waters. Ernie seemed to swim even faster, pulling himself smoothly over the tops of the waves. One of Colin's arms surfaced, then sank again.

Everyone on the beach had run down to the shoreline. They watched in silence, then let out a spontaneous, hopeful cheer as Ernie reached Colin and began pulling him back to the beach.

It seemed to Amy that it took forever to get him back.

HOW I BROKE UP WITH ERNIE

Finally Ernie pulled Colin up on the beach, rolled him over on his back, and began pushing hard on his chest. A little water spewed out of Colin's mouth, and he quickly sat up. The crowd of relieved onlookers cheered again.

"I'm okay. Really. I'm okay. You don't have to do that," he said. His face was bright red, almost purple. Seaweed was tangled in his hair.

"Just trying to get the water out," Ernie said, backing off Colin. "You sure you're okay?"

"Yeah. I just had a cramp. I could've made it, but I got a cramp." Colin looked very embarrassed.

The crowd started to break up. Ernie helped Colin up.

"I'm fine. Really," Colin protested.

Amy came running up. "I—I was so worried. Everyone was. But you're okay?"

Colin flashed her his 230-tooth grin. His face was still purple though. He was trembling all over. "I'm okay. But I guess it was a close one. Ernie saved my life."

He shook Ernie's hand. "Thanks, I owe you one."

"Aw, I was going for a swim anyway," Ernie said with exaggerated modesty.

"I just had a cramp," Colin repeated for some reason. "That's all it was. Just a cramp. Come over to my blanket. Okay? I'm so grateful, Ernie. Really."

"Okay," Ernie said, putting his big arm around Colin's narrow shoulders.

Colin and Ernie walked to the blanket, talking about the waves and the undertow. Amy followed behind. They seemed to have forgotten about her.

Ernie plopped down on the blanket first. Colin wrapped himself up in a striped beach towel, then sat down next to Ernie. They hadn't left any room for Amy. She sat down on the sand beside Colin.

"I'm starting to warm up," Colin said.

"You're not really cold. It's just shock," Ernie said.

"I can't believe you saved my life," Colin said, shaking his head. He shook hands with Ernie again.

Ernie pulled away and picked up his magazine. "I can't either," he said. "I just hoped I could get there in time."

"The undertow was powerful. It was pulling to the left," Colin said.

"It was pulling left and right. That was the problem," Ernie added.

They went on talking about their adventure for a long while, congratulating and thanking each other, patting each other on the back, and then teasing and joking about the entire episode. Amy was ignored entirely.

Finally she got up off the sand and stretched. "Think I'll go find Reg," she said. She yawned meaningfully.

"Bye," Colin said. "See you soon." He and Ernie continued their animated conversation.

Amy wandered away from everyone. She didn't see Regina. Maybe I'll just go home, she thought dispiritedly.

"You're Amy Wayne, aren't you?"

A girl Amy didn't really know but who looked vaguely familiar was standing in front of her. "Yes, I am. You're—"

"I'm Julia. Ernie's cousin."

"Oh. Right. Sorry," Amy said.

"I heard you broke up with Ernie," Julia said, her small, black eyes piercing into Amy's.

Amy wasn't expecting that. "Well, y-yes," she stammered.

"It isn't really any of my business," Julia said, frowning hard at Amy. "But if you broke up with Ernie, it isn't very nice of you to keep forcing him to tag along with you everywhere you go."

Chapter
9

"Oooh, gross!" Lisa Norman squealed.

"It's not gross. It's an anchovy." Jenny Herman raised the dark, slivery object high between her two fingers, moving it closer to Lisa's face.

"Put it down, Jenny. It's gross. And it's gross of you to pick it up like that." Lisa was the authority among Amy's friends as to what was gross. To her, just about everything was.

"You know what's gross about it?" Jenny said, her blue eyes sparkling in the candlelight, her devilish smile hidden in the shadows. "What's gross about it is—it's alive!"

She tossed the anchovy onto Lisa's neck.

"YAAAAIII!" Lisa ripped it off her neck and tossed it to the floor.

"Hey, come on— What kind of party is this?" Amy complained.

"Happy birthday," Regina muttered.

"That's right. It's my birthday party. So how

come you're throwing anchovies at each other?"
Amy asked.

"I didn't. She did," Lisa whined.

"What kind of Sweet Sixteen party is this, anyway?" Regina echoed Amy.

"It's not a real Sweet Sixteen party," Amy said.
"That would be too corny."

"Even for you," someone muttered.

Amy didn't seem to hear. "It's a Semisweet
Sixteen party," she announced.

"That's your idea of a joke—right?" Regina said
as sarcastic as ever.

"Yeah, I guess," Amy admitted.

"Well, I guess it's funnier than throwing anchovies," Regina said.

"Don't knock it unless you've tried it," Jenny
said, pulling another anchovy off the remains of the
pizza in the center of the table.

"You're my best friends in the world," Amy
gushed, trying to get the party more upbeat.

"That's the most depressing thing I've heard all
night," Regina cracked. Everyone laughed.

"How come you're not spending your birthday
with Colin?" Risa Gould teased from the far end of
the table.

"Yeah. How come?" Lisa repeated.

"I might be seeing him later," Amy said coyly.

"He's a fox," someone muttered.

"Ugh," someone else said quietly.

"Are we having cake? I want to put on at least
another twenty pounds tonight," Jenny groaned.

"It would look good on you," Regina said.

Jenny pretended to be offended. "What's that
supposed to mean, Giraffe Breath?"

"What did you call me?"

The doorbell rang. Amy gratefully ran to answer it.

A man in a green uniform and cap was waiting at the front door with a bouquet of blue and white helium balloons. "Wow!" Amy was delighted. "Who are these from?"

"I just deliver 'em," the guy said gloomily.

Everyone cheered when Amy walked back into the dining room with them. "Let's open them up and inhale the helium!" Jenny suggested.

"That's gross," Lisa predictably declared.

"We'll all talk funny. It'll be hysterical," Risa said.

"You already talk funny," Regina told her. She turned to Amy. "That was really thoughtful of Colin. I might have to change my opinion of him." Then she quickly added, "But I doubt it."

Everyone laughed again.

The balloons, bobbing up at the ceiling, were definitely making the party a bit more festive. Amy had refused to decorate at all since it was only a Semisweet Sixteen party.

She pulled open the card attached to the balloon strings and eagerly read it. Her face sank. She looked as if she might cry.

"They're from Ernie," she said, her voice barely a whisper.

"Ernie? Amy, you didn't tell us you were still seeing him too," Risa teased.

"Oh, yes," Amy said wearily. "I'm still seeing him. All the time."

"She sees him—like spots before her eyes," Regina added.

"I broke up with him three weeks ago. But he's here almost every night for dinner. He comes over to play with the boys. He's going to work for my father this summer. Whenever I leave the house, he—he's . . ." Her voice trailed off in misery.

The room grew silent for a moment.

"Hey, is someone talking about me? My ears are red!" Ernie burst into the room. He had dressed up for the party. He was wearing a clean gray T-shirt and reasonably clean running pants.

"Ernie—" Amy started to scream. Then she remembered she was holding his balloon bouquet. "Uh—the balloons. Thank you, but—"

"You like 'em? It was real expensive. But I thought, what the heck."

He sat down at the far end of the table, squeezing in between Risa and Jenny. The girls all laughed.

"Ernie, you've got to be the first guy in Seaview to crash a Sweet Sixteen party," Regina told him, rolling her eyes in disapproval.

"I'm not particular." He grinned, his eyes crinkling. "Slide the pizza down, Lisa. You've had too much already." He laughed as if he had just made the wittiest joke in history.

"For sure," Lisa said. "At least *my* nickname isn't Bear."

"Are bears an endangered species?" Risa asked.

"Not around this house," Regina cracked.

Amy gave her a weak smile. Bear was too busy glomming down pizza to respond. "Hey—what happened to all the anchovies?" he complained.

The party broke up a few minutes later. Everyone suddenly had a million things to do since it was a Saturday afternoon. "A bunch of party poopers,"

Ernie said, clicking his teeth, reaching for the pizza remains Jenny had left behind on her plate. "Great party, though, Amy. Great party."

"Ernie—really," Amy said. She didn't have the energy to scream at him. But she knew she had to get through to him somehow, had to make him realize that he must get out of her life.

She had broken up with him, after all.

She left him at the table and walked into the den. A few seconds later he followed her, still chewing. "Got any more?" he asked. "Your friends are big eaters. They didn't leave much."

Amy let her anger build slowly. She wasn't going to say a word until she was ready to explode. Then she was really going to let Ernie have it once and for all.

"Oh. Wow. I almost forgot," Ernie said, slapping his forehead really hard. He handed her a small package wrapped in gold foil wrap.

"What's this?" Amy asked suspiciously. She was busy letting her anger build. Why was he handing her a birthday present?

"Open it."

"Ernie—no." She pushed it toward him.

He pushed it back into her hand. "Go ahead. Open it."

She opened it. Inside the box was a beautiful pendant. It appeared to be made of real silver.

"No," she said, shoving it back into his hand. "Take it back."

"I gave it to you," he said, his eyes crinkling. He put it back in her hand. "Happy birthday."

"No," she insisted. "I won't take it. No. I won't.

Ernie—don't you understand? I broke up with you."

"Try it on. Go ahead," Ernie insisted, trying to open the clasp with his big, stubby fingers.

"No. I broke up with you. It's over. It's all over between us."

Ernie shrugged. For the first time, he looked a little embarrassed. But it was only because he couldn't get the clasp open. "I can still bring you a birthday present, can't I?" he said softly. He put a hand on her shoulder. He squeezed her shoulder tenderly.

"No. No. No!" she pulled away from him. "I'm not taking it, Ernie. Take your present back. I want you to finally understand. I broke up with you. That's it. It's over!"

She grabbed the pendant and flung it at him. It hit him in the chest and clinked onto the tile floor.

Ernie looked more surprised than hurt. He bent over and carefully picked up the pendant. He replaced it in the gift box. Then he shrugged, and without looking at her, walked quickly from the den.

Finally, Amy thought. Finally.

She took a deep breath.

Freedom!

She went back to the dining room and started to clear away the dirty plates. But she was too impatient to clean up now. She had to get out of the house, go celebrate her birthday, celebrate her *freedom*.

After changing into tan short shorts, a white sleeveless top, and sandals, she hurried to the beach. The sun spread its warmth everywhere. The sky was a brilliant, glowing blue. Amy glowed too. She felt so good, she practically skipped the whole way.

She actually felt a little guilty for feeling so good. She didn't really want to hurt Ernie, after all. He was a good guy and everything. But hurting him seemed to be the only way to get through to him.

Poor guy.

But this was no time to think about him. Amy realized that now she'd be able to think about him less and less. And concentrate on other people—such as Colin.

The silver and tan Saab was parked on Dune Road. That meant that Colin was on the beach. Amy took off her sandals and, carrying them in one hand, started to jog across the sand.

The beach was crowded. The waves were low and calm, and a few brave souls had ventured in despite the freezing water temperature. "Almost summer," Amy thought. "This could be the greatest summer of my life!"

She spotted Colin at the edge of the stone jetty, listening to his CD boom box. "Colin, hi!" She came running up and impetuously kissed him on the cheek.

He looked surprised. "Hi. What was that for?"

"For—I don't know. For my birthday."

She was a little disappointed in his unenthusiastic response. But he quickly began to brighten. "Hey, that's great, Amy. Happy birthday."

"Yeah." She smiled at him. He smiled at her. She was out of breath from running across the sand.

"Nice day, huh?" he said finally. "Nice day for a birthday."

"For sure."

"Want to walk on the beach?"

"Yes," she said. "That's a great idea. Let's go for a long, long walk."

He laughed at her enthusiasm. "Okay."

He took her hand and they climbed over the jetty, heading away from the crowded part of the beach. His hand felt strong and warm in hers. The sun seemed to beam down harder. Amy felt warm and happy all over.

What a day. What a summer. What a life . . .

"Hey, wait up!" a familiar voice called. "Wait up!"

They turned to see Ernie running at top speed to join them.

Chapter
10

"Help me peel carrots," Mrs. Wayne said. "I'm making a beef stew."

"Peel carrots? I don't think I have the strength," Amy moaned. She was sitting on a kitchen stool, staring at the clothes spinning round and round through the window on the washing machine.

"Amy—" Her mother sounded worried. "That isn't the TV, you know."

"I know," Amy said gloomily, not looking up. "It doesn't matter."

"Okay. Let's forget the carrots." Her mother pulled a stool over and sat down next to her.

Uh-oh, Amy told herself. It's heart-to-heart time. She thought of getting up and leaving the room. But she quickly changed her mind. Maybe talking to her mother wasn't such a bad idea.

"What's your problem?" Mrs. Wayne asked gently. "Is it Ernie?"

"How'd you know?" Amy was always surprised

when her mother knew more than Amy thought she did.

"I know."

"He won't leave me alone," Amy wailed. "I broke up with him, but he won't leave me alone. He's everywhere I go. Everywhere!"

"Why do you think he's doing it?" her mother asked with real concern. "Ernie isn't a stupid person."

"Yeah, that's true," Amy agreed.

"He likes to play dumb sometimes," her mother continued. "He likes people to think he's just a big, amiable all-around guy. But Ernie's pretty smart. So, I don't think he's staying in your life because he doesn't understand that you broke up with him."

Amy thought about it. Her mother was right. Ernie wasn't that stupid. And he wasn't in shock either.

That left only one explanation.

"He's just trying to trick me into going back with him!" Amy declared, narrowing her eyes in anger. "It's all a trick, a plot! He's deliberately hanging around me so that no one else can! He's acting so innocent, but it's all part of his plan! He's trying to—to ruin my life!"

She didn't realize it, but she was shouting now. "All this time I've been worried about his feelings. Poor Ernie, I thought. Poor, hurt Ernie. And all the while, he's been trying to trick me, deliberately trying to force me to go back with him!"

"What's all the shouting?" Mr. Wayne came rushing into the kitchen.

Mrs. Wayne waved him away. "Amy's just a little upset, that's all."

Mr. Wayne stared at Amy for a long while. "I've got a great idea," he said. "We've all been a little out of sorts lately. I've got an idea that will get us feeling chipper again!"

A few days later found all the Waynes trudging through the woods.

"Don't put the pack down there. Hear me? Don't put the pack down there!" Amy's dad cried.

Michael put the pack down in the mud.

"I told you not to put the pack down. Can't you hear? Am I talking to the trees?"

Michael and Max thought the idea of talking to the trees was very funny. They laughed and hit each other. Then Max put his pack down in the mud too.

"Pick it up! Pick it up!" Mr. Wayne yelled.

"Talking to the trees!" the boys exclaimed, giggling happily.

"Pick up your packs, boys," Mrs. Wayne said quietly but firmly, pronouncing each word very carefully the way she always did when she was angry. "They're in the mud."

"But it's too heavy," Max complained.

"Yeah. Too heavy," Michael agreed.

"We don't have much farther to go," Mr. Wayne said, shifting the tent and the long tent poles from one shoulder to the other. "So get your packs out of the mud."

"But it's muddy everywhere!" Max whined.

"Yeah, I guess," Mr. Wayne said, frowning. "I didn't expect it to rain so hard yesterday." He suddenly turned to Amy. "You're awfully quiet today."

Amy felt like a pack mule under the bulging blue

sleeping bag she carried strapped to her back. "I just don't understand why we're out here in the woods, tromping through the mud when we have a perfectly nice house we can stay in and a TV set we could be watching."

"Thanks for your enthusiasm." Mr. Wayne looked really hurt.

"You know your father planned this camping trip just for you," Amy's mother said quietly. Mrs. Wayne hated camping trips. She hardly ever went into the backyard. But today she was being a good sport.

"That's right," Mr. Wayne said, pouting. "This is just what you need, isn't it? It's always great to get away from everyone and everything, and just be alone together in the woods."

"But we're not alone. There are bears here too. Right?" Michael added.

"Bears? Real, live bears?" Max didn't look too pleased to hear this news.

"Yeah. Bears," Michael said gleefully. "Listen. You can hear them."

Max listened very carefully. The woods were silent. "I don't hear any bears," he told his brother.

"They're whispering," Michael said. "Bears always whisper before they *attack!*" With that, he leapt onto Max's back.

"Cut it out! Cut it *out!*"

"It was nice of you to think of us, Daddy," Amy said, pulling the boys apart. "But maybe thinking about camping is more fun than actually doing it."

Mrs. Wayne laughed, but Mr. Wayne didn't think it was funny. "Pick up your gear," he told the twins. "Come on. Let's try to have some fun and enjoy this, okay? I think there's a flat campground just past those trees."

Grumbling and shoving each other, the twins picked up their heavy packs.

They made it through the trees with only a few minor incidents. A twig on a low tree branch scratched Max's cheek. And Mrs. Wayne twisted her ankle, tripping over an upraised tree root.

The sun was settling behind a clump of fir trees when they reached the campground. A flock of Canada geese flew overhead in perfect formation, honking loudly.

"It's so beautiful out here," Amy admitted. Now that the long hike was over, she was starting to cheer up. "It really was a nice idea, Daddy. With all of my problems and stuff, I really did need a few days away."

Mr. Wayne gave her a pleased smile. He set to work putting up the tent. The sun had completely disappeared behind the tall firs by the time he'd finished.

"We'd better get some firewood before it's pitch-black out here," he said, buttoning the top button of his plaid wool lumberjack coat. "Come on, boys. Come with me. You can collect kindling."

"What's a kindling?" Max asked.

"It's like a bear, only bigger!" Michael told him.

"No, it isn't," Max insisted. But he wasn't sure.

"Stop teasing your brother, Michael," Mr. Wayne said.

"Who's teasing?" Michael shrugged. "I'm serious!"

They followed Mr. Wayne into the woods.

Amy and her mom set to work unrolling the

sleeping bags and unpacking the dinner supplies. High in the trees, birds declared that it was evening. A gust of wind made the new spring leaves whisper and shake.

A small brown squirrel came out from behind a tree and boldly crept forward to investigate them. The squirrel stood up on two legs and held out its front paws, as if begging.

Mrs. Wayne tossed the squirrel a cracker, but it ran away without collecting it.

Amy laughed. "This might be fun after all," she told her mother. "It smells so good out here. Everything smells so fresh and real."

"I'm glad you're starting to enjoy it," Mrs. Wayne said, smoothing out one of the boys' bright blue sleeping bags. "You're always so busy. We don't get that much time to spend together anymore."

"I know," Amy said softly.

A short while later they heard footsteps crunching toward them. Mr. Wayne, loaded down with firewood, stepped out of the trees, followed by the twins, who were each carrying handfuls of sticks and twigs, followed by another figure, carrying a massive load of sticks and twigs.

"Hey, look who I found in the woods!" Mr. Wayne declared. "It's Ernie!"

Chapter
11

"Has Colin asked you to the spring dance?" Regina asked.

Amy sighed. "No, he hasn't. He's probably afraid that if he asks me, he has to ask Ernie, too." She sighed again. She'd been doing a lot of long and despairing sighing lately.

They were up in Amy's room, Amy on the bed, Regina in the chair by the window, tossing one of Amy's stuffed pigs back and forth and bemoaning their fate as the end of the school year rapidly approached.

"Marty Webb asked me to the dance," Regina said, rolling her eyes.

"He did? What did you say?"

"Amy, what could I say? Marty Webb only comes up to my kneecaps!"

"So what did you say?"

"I told him I'd think about it."

Amy laughed. "You'd make a cute couple."

"Right. I'd have to pick him up to dance with him!" Regina laughed too.

"Why are we laughing?" Amy asked.

"Because we're miserable?"

"Probably. Listen, Reg, I called you over because I had an idea. But I know you're going to say no."

"Okay. No," Regina said. She squeezed the stuffed pig hard. It honked. "When are you going to get rid of these babyish pigs?" she asked.

"I don't know. I still like them," Amy said defensively. "Don't try to change the subject."

"I'm not changing the subject. I already said no."

"Come on, Reg."

Something about the desperate look in Amy's eyes made Regina relent. "What is it, Amy? I can't lend you any money. I spent all my money on that green T-shirt dress that looks so disgusting on me."

"That dress looks great on you, Reg."

"I know. I was just fishing for a compliment."

"Reg, listen. You've got to do me a really big favor. I wouldn't ask you if I wasn't truly desperate."

"The suspense is killing me."

"Reg, you're the only one I can turn to. You've got to help me with Ernie. I want you to ask Ernie out."

These words were greeted by a lengthy silence. Regina stared across the room at Amy without moving or blinking an eye. Finally she said, "What?"

"Ask Ernie out," Amy repeated timidly. "Just for one date?"

"But why, Amy?"

"Because if you ask him out, he'll realize that you wouldn't ask him without asking me first, and I obviously said it was okay, so he'll realize that it's okay with me if he goes out with other girls, and that'll make him realize that we're not going out together anymore."

"That makes perfect sense," Regina said, tossing the stuffed pig up to the ceiling. "What you really want is for me to ask him out so you won't have him hanging around for one night."

"No. It's more of a symbol. Don't you see?"

"Sort of."

"So will you do it?"

"Of course not." Regina stood up and stretched.

"Please, Reg. I'll beg if I have to. I'll never ask another favor. I'll be your slave for a year. Really."

"Keep going," Regina said, collapsing back into the chair. "I like the direction you're heading in."

"So you'll do it? You'll ask him out."

"I'm going to be sorry," Regina said, putting her finger to her head as if it were a gun.

"It's just one night of your life," Amy said, relaxing a little, so relieved that Regina was agreeing to her plan. "And I know it'll really make a difference. It'll force Ernie to finally accept things. He isn't a bad guy, you know. He's really kinda sweet. Just ask him to go to the movies or something. You might have a pretty good time."

"Stop it, Amy," Regina said firmly. "I've already said I'll do it. Now you don't have to sell Ernie to me like a used car."

Amy happily leapt off the bed, walked over to the phone, and lifted up the receiver. "Call him now.

Oh, please. Do it now. You're the best friend a person ever had, Reg."

Reg slowly climbed up from the chair, swinging her long, black hair behind her with a quick toss of her head. "I know, I know," she muttered. She took the receiver from Amy. "You think this is going to help?"

"I do. I really do."

"You really *are* desperate!" Regina exclaimed. "What's Ernie's number?"

Amy told her. Regina punched the numbers. The two girls stood frozen there for a long while, Regina leaning on Amy's desk with the receiver on her ear, Amy a step to her right.

"No answer. No one home," Regina said finally. She shrugged and set the receiver down lightly.

Amy looked very disappointed. "Where would he be? It's ten o'clock at night." A thought flashed through her mind. "Follow me," she told Regina.

The two girls walked downstairs. There was Ernie sitting on the living room couch, looking at the sports section of the newspaper.

"Where else?" Amy said aloud.

Ernie looked up, crushed the newspaper onto his lap, and smiled at them. "Hi ya."

"Hi ya," Regina repeated. She gave Amy a doubtful look. Amy gave her a polite shove.

"Ernie, I didn't know you were here," Amy said.

"Yeah," Ernie replied, still smiling. He clicked his teeth. "I was talking to your dad. But I guess he went to bed."

There was a long silence while they listened to the house creak.

"Regina wants to talk to you," Amy said, looking very nervous.

"She does?" Ernie looked surprised.

Regina sat down at the edge of the couch and made a face at Amy.

"See you later," Amy said. She turned quickly and hurried up the stairs.

Back in her room, Amy paced back and forth for a while. But the room really wasn't long enough for effective pacing. She sat down at her desk, got up, went to the doorway, listened for a while, heard Ernie and Regina talking quietly, too quietly to make out any of the words, and tried pacing again.

"Maybe it *is* time to get rid of my pig collection," she decided. She got a large shopping bag down from the top of her closet and began tossing her prized stuffed pigs into it one by one.

When the shopping bag was full, she decided she wasn't ready to get rid of her pig collection after all. She sat down on the floor beside the shopping bag and began pulling out pigs one by one.

Before Amy had finished getting all of the pigs back onto the night table, Regina entered the room. She was smiling, but it wasn't the kind of smile Amy had expected. It wasn't the kind of smile a person who was about to go out on a date with Ernie might wear.

"Well?" Amy climbed to her feet, tossed a pig back into the bag. "Did you make a date?"

"No," Regina said softly, standing over Amy, still wearing that annoying, enigmatic smile.

"You didn't ask him?"

"Of course I asked him," Regina told her, a little offended. "He said no."

"No?"

"No. He was very sweet. He said he didn't want to go out with me because he's still working really hard to get over you."

"Working hard to get over me?" Amy screamed. "Working hard!" She suddenly lost it. "That's how he gets over me? By sitting in my living room twenty-four hours a day?"

"Ssshhh. He'll hear you," Regina whispered. "He's still down there reading the newspaper."

Chapter 12

Amy staggered to her locker lugging about two hundred pounds of textbooks in her book bag. What a day! Two surprise quizzes, an oral book report (on a book she had only read the first chapter of), and a history exam. She couldn't wait to throw her books down and get home to rest.

"That exam was gross," Lisa Norman, looking as exhausted as Amy, said, her book bag bumping Amy from the side, almost sending her sprawling into the water fountain.

"Sorry. So how'd you do?"

"Okay, I guess," Amy said. Her head felt as if it were filled with feathers, a feeling she always got after writing and concentrating hard for an hour.

"Only two more weeks of school." Lisa sighed. "And we're only up to World War One. How's Mr. Maloney gonna squeeze World War Two, Korea, and Vietnam into just two weeks?"

"He'll find a way," Amy groaned.

"Gross," Lisa said. She gave Amy a wave, bumped her again with her bulging book bag, and continued down the crowded hallway.

It was easy to tell which kids had just come from the history exam. They all wore the same dazed expression as Amy. They walked silently, blinking and shaking their heads. The other kids were laughing and joking, talking loudly and enthusiastically, slamming their books in their lockers and eagerly heading out for home or their afterschool jobs.

Amy finally reached her locker and pressed her warm forehead against the cool metal. "I ran out of ink twice," someone said behind her.

Startled, Amy turned around to find Regina wearing the same battle-weary look. "Two pens," Regina said. "Brand new ballpoint pens. They both ran out of ink."

"How much did you write?" Amy asked.

"Fourteen pages."

"Come on, Regina. I don't believe you. You wrote fourteen pages in an hour?"

"Uh-huh. I didn't know anything, so I had to write a lot. If I had read the material, I probably could've gotten away with four or five pages."

Amy laughed.

"I'm totally serious," Regina said.

"Totally," Amy repeated. She looked past Regina, and her expression changed. "Here comes Colin."

Regina turned around. "He's smiling. I guess he didn't take the exam."

Colin gave them both a cheerful greeting. He looked very springlike in pleated chinos and a madras button-down shirt. "How's it going?"

Regina and Amy both groaned.

"Oh. You took the history exam. We don't have ours till next week."

"I used up two pens," Regina told him.

"You should use a fountain pen," Colin told her. "That way you can just refill it." He pulled a green fountain pen from his shirt pocket and showed it to her.

"There's always one kid in every class who uses a fountain pen," Regina sneered. "I can't use one. I press too hard."

"It takes practice," Colin said seriously. He didn't seem to realize that Regina had just insulted him.

But Amy did. She gave Regina a dirty look.

"Guess I'll be running," Regina said, getting the hint. "See you guys later. Nice pen, Colin."

"Thanks," Colin said, replacing it carefully in his shirt pocket.

They watched Regina hurry off down the hall. Amy pressed her head against the locker again.

"Bad day?" Colin asked.

"Two quizzes, a book report, and the history exam."

"Bad day," he agreed. "Can I ask you something?"

She turned to face him. "Of course."

"Well—" He looked nervous. His ears turned red.

"Ask me anything," Amy said, getting curious.

"Anything?" That seemed to strike Colin funny. He guffawed for a while, shaking his head.

He's even handsome when he giggles, Amy thought. She leaned back against the locker and waited for him to continue. "What did you want to ask me?" she asked finally.

"Well, I was wondering if—if you don't have a date—I mean—if you'd like to go to the spring dance with me?"

Colin's ears were bright scarlet. He must have known it. He dropped his book bag and started rubbing them.

"I'd love to," Amy said, giving him a warm smile. Her head seemed to clear. She felt fine again. "Thank you for asking me."

"You'll go?" Colin asked, sounding more surprised than he should. He quickly answered his own question. "Oh. Right. Of course you'll go. You said yes."

"Yes," Amy said again. "It'll be fun. I have a dress all picked out."

"So do I," Colin said. "No! I mean—" His ears looked as if they were about to combust spontaneously into flames. "What's the theme of the dance this year?" he asked, quickly changing the subject.

"There isn't one," she said. "They couldn't decide."

"No theme?"

"No. The student council took a vote, and it came out a tie. So they decided not to have a theme this year."

"Oh, well," Colin said. A short while later he repeated it. "Oh, well." Then he put a hand against the wall and leaned closer to Amy. "Listen, I'm sorry. I know I'm acting like a jerk. I guess I was just nervous about asking you to the dance."

"You shouldn't be nervous," Amy said, giving

him her warmest, most reassuring smile. "I really like you, Colin."

His ears flamed again. "I really like you too, Amy." He leaned even closer and kissed her quickly on the lips.

She pulled back, surprised. Then she felt embarrassed that she had pulled away. She turned away from him, pulled open her locker door—and let out a bloodcurdling scream.

Ernie was inside the locker.

"Gotcha!" he said.

He flashed her a triumphant grin, squeezed out of the locker, and trotted off without saying another word.

Amy and Colin stood in silence watching Ernie until he turned the corner.

"What's his problem?" Colin asked.

Amy shook her head. Her heartbeat was beginning to return to normal. "I don't think he accepts the fact that you and I are going out." She wearily tossed her books into the bottom of the now-empty locker.

"Would you like me to talk to him?" Colin asked.

Would I! Amy thought. I'd have liked you to talk to him six weeks ago! If you hadn't been such a wimp about Ernie all this time, I wouldn't have him waiting for me inside my locker like some kind of a maniac!

That's what she thought. But what she said was, "That would be really great."

"Okay. I'll go catch up with him right now," Colin said.

"Great. That's great. It just might work. If you lay it on the line to him, it might just work."

"Right. I'll lay it on the line," Colin said, a look of hard determination forming on his usually soft face. He turned and trotted off down the hall.

"Colin, don't be too tough on him!" Amy called.

"I'll try!" Colin shouted back before he disappeared around the corner.

Amy was a block from her house when curiosity got the better of her. She was dying to know how Colin's man-to-man talk with Ernie was going. It was all she could think about as she walked home. She didn't even think about the spring dance or telling Regina that Colin had finally asked her.

Now, where would Colin and Ernie be talking? she asked herself. The Snack Bar, she quickly decided.

The little snack bar called The Snack Bar was just two blocks from Seaview High. Amy turned around and began walking there as quickly as she could.

She didn't plan to go inside. She just wanted to take a quick peek through the window. She was sure she could tell in a glance how the talk was going by the looks on the boys' faces.

A few minutes later she was standing in front of the window, taking her quick glance. Then she took another. And another not-so-quick glance.

Sure enough, there were Ernie and Colin having their man-to-man talk in the second booth. But the talk did not appear to be going as Amy had hoped—or imagined it.

The two boys appeared to be having a great time. They both had mile-high ice-cream sundaes in front of them. They were laughing and slapping the table.

Ernie reached across the table and gave Colin a playful punch on the shoulder, and both boys exploded in more laughter.

"They're having a blast!" Amy told herself, staring at them in disbelief through the smeared glass, not even bothering just to glance.

When she finally turned away, they were still joking and laughing and slapping each other high-fives.

"Oh, well, back to the drawing board," Amy said sadly. "I'm never going to get rid of Ernie. Never."

Chapter 13

One of the most exciting things about the spring dance was that it wasn't held in the Seaview gym. This year, the dance was being held at Rage, an adult disco and dance club in the nearby town of West Beach.

Amy felt great as she and Colin stepped into the swirling lights of the multilevel club and looked around. She was ready for the most wonderful evening of her life.

She knew she looked wonderful in the flowing, satiny white dress with its short-waisted, glittery, black-sequined jacket. Just clingy enough, just sparkly enough, just light and romantic enough for dancing all night.

Colin looked wonderful too. A little too formal maybe in the white dinner jacket. But she knew he'd loosen up once they got out on the dance floor.

The dance floor! It was enormous. And it was raised up a foot from the rest of the room. Blinking strobe lights of red and purple played over it, moving in time to the music. Above the dance floor, a gigantic wide-screen TV played throbbingly loud videos. The videos were repeated on the far wall on dozens of smaller screen TVs. And all around, the sound of the never-ending dance music boomed from dozens of speakers cranked up all the way so that the walls vibrated, the ceilings echoed, and the floor shook beneath their feet.

"The music!" Amy declared to Colin, deliriously happy already. "It goes right through you. You can feel it in your whole body. It's like you become part of the music!"

"What?" Colin asked, cupping his ear.

"It's fabulous!" Amy gushed. "Isn't it fabulous? The lights make you feel so—so surrounded!"

"What?"

Colin was having trouble hearing her even though she was shouting in his ear.

Amy waved to Lisa and her date, and pulled Colin toward the dance floor. "Let's check out the food first," Colin yelled.

A bar ran the entire length of the dance floor. Amy saw breads and cheese, a crystal punch bowl filled with a dark red liquid with orange slices floating on the top, bowls of pretzels and potato chips, and an enormous white, three-layer cake.

"Come on, I want to dance!" Amy pleaded. She was too excited to stand around. "I'm sure you're a terrific dancer."

Colin gave her a confident grin. "Well, yes, I am pretty good. I had private lessons."

"Hi, everybody!"

It was Regina. She was wearing a long, slinky red

dress and long, dangly red plastic earrings. She was accompanied by Marty Webb, who was wearing black, high-heeled boots so that he came up nearly to Regina's shoulder.

"Regina, isn't this fabulous?" Amy cried.

"If you like lights and colors and excitement," Regina said. But even she looked excited.

"I wouldn't want their electric bill!" Marty said and then laughed as if he'd made the best joke ever.

"What?" Colin asked.

"This sound system even makes Madonna sound good!" Regina cracked.

Amy had her eyes closed and was moving in time to the insistent beat.

"I like your car," Marty said to Colin.

"What?"

"Your car. It's really gear."

"No. It's a Saab," Colin said, pretending he could hear.

"My dad lets me drive our Mitsubishi," Marty shouted. "He said if I could pronounce it, I could drive it." He burst into hysterical laughter again.

Colin forced a smile.

Amy continued to sway to the music.

"Isn't the cake gross?" Lisa asked, appearing suddenly from the dark swirls of purple and red.

"I think it's beautiful," Amy said. "I think everything's beautiful tonight."

"Watch out, Colin," Regina warned. "If she starts to float away, pull her down by the ankles."

"What?"

"The music is so loud, you can't hear yourself think," Lisa griped.

"I don't want to think," Amy said dreamily. "I

just want to dance." She grabbed Colin by the hand and tugged. "Now."

"I can take a hint," Colin said, smiling at Regina and following Amy.

"Break a leg," Marty said and laughed like a hyena.

Amy pulled Colin up onto the dance floor. The lights were absolutely dizzying. The floor shook under her feet in rhythm with the pulsating synthesized drumbeat.

They started to dance.

Colin moved slowly to the music. But he quickly picked up the rhythm. Amy laughed from sheer delight. He hadn't lied. He was a terrific dancer.

He gave her a warm smile as he moved, and she returned it. Then she closed her eyes and let the music take her.

She was in her own world now, dancing with the music and only with the music.

I am the music and the music is me, she thought.

She danced, smiling happily, ecstatically, her eyes closed, feeling the rhythm, feeling the power of the magnificent sound system, feeling happy, young, and excitingly alive.

What a night. What a beautiful, romantic, unforgettable night!

When she opened her eyes, she saw Ernie.

He was bounding across the dance floor toward her, carrying two glasses of punch, a wide, eager grin on his face.

No!

This can't be happening!

I can't take it anymore! she thought.

I *won't* take this anymore!

He's not going to spoil this dance for me. This is the happiest night of my life, and I won't let him ruin it!

Colin looked surprised as Amy turned and hopped off the dance floor. Then Colin saw Ernie. He followed Ernie as Ernie followed Amy toward the bar.

"No, Ernie, no!" Amy screamed. "You can't do this to me!"

Kids near the bar turned to see what the commotion was. A few couples on the dance floor stopped dancing.

"But, Amy—" Ernie pleaded.

"I broke up with you, Ernie!" Amy screamed, not caring who heard her, not caring about anything at all except finally getting through to Ernie.

"Do you hear me? Do you understand English? I broke up with you. We don't go together anymore!"

"But Amy. I—"

By this time everyone had stopped dancing and had turned to stare at Amy. Colin tried to take Amy's arm, but she pulled away. She was in such a state of fury, she didn't even see him.

"You don't have the right to follow me here, Ernie! You don't have the right! I broke up with you! Do you understand?"

"But, Amy, I—" He nearly spilled the two drinks in his hands.

"I'm going to make sure you remember!" Amy screamed. "I'm going to teach you to leave me alone *once and for all!*" She ran to the bar.

"Amy—stop!" someone yelled.

But it was too late to stop.

The tall, white cake was in her hands.

And a second later she was dumping it over Ernie's head.

The music stopped. No one was laughing now. Everyone was horrified.

Amy struggled to catch her breath. She was breathing so hard, she was wheezing.

Ernie wiped chunks of chocolate cake off his face. The gooey white icing formed a helmet on top of his head. Cake and icing had fallen inside his jacket. His white tuxedo shirt was smeared with cake. Clumps of cake sat on the tops of his shoes.

No one said anything. No one moved.

Ernie slowly pulled his jacket off. He used it to wipe off his face and hair.

Then he looked up at Amy, icing still clinging to his eyebrows.

"I was just bringing my date some punch," he said quietly.

Amy's mouth dropped open in disbelief. "What?"

"I said I was just bringing my date some punch."

"You mean you weren't—"

"I don't think you know her," Ernie said. "She just transferred here from upstate."

"You mean you— You mean she—" Amy had to lean against the bar to keep from falling over.

A girl with curly blond hair, wearing a sleeveless, pale green dress, took a step forward. She was staring daggers at Amy.

"Ingrid, this is Amy," Ernie said. "Amy, this is Ingrid."

Ernie used his jacket to wipe more icing from his hair.

Amy had never felt so embarrassed, so completely mortified and humiliated in all her life.

What should she do now? What *could* she do?

She looked around for Colin. He had vanished.

Was that him slipping out the back exit?

She turned back to Ingrid. "Uh—pleased to meet you," she said, giving her a warm, friendly handshake.

Ingrid made a face and looked down at her hand. It was smeared with sticky white icing.

Chapter
14

A few days later Amy and Regina were walking behind the school grounds. It was a perfect spring afternoon, high white clouds dotting a startlingly blue sky, birds chirping in the tall oak trees that lined the teachers' parking lot, the jingle of an ice-cream truck a few blocks away.

"Isn't that Marty Webb on the tennis court?" Amy asked, squinting to see better.

"Yeah. Look. Isn't that a riot? He has to stand on tiptoes to shake hands over the net." Regina chuckled at her own joke.

Amy shook her head. "Come on, Reg. He isn't that short."

"Oh, yeah? After the dance Saturday night, he sprained his neck trying to kiss me goodnight."

"You're impossible," Amy said. She sighed. She'd been doing a lot of sighing since the dance.

Regina picked up on her friend's sadness. "Sorry. I didn't mean to bring up the dance."

"That's okay," Amy said softly. "You can bring up the dance. In fact, you can bring it up once a day. Remind me of what an idiot I am."

Regina stopped and looked at Amy in surprise. "Do I detect actual bitterness?" she exclaimed. "Hey, that's not your personality at all."

"It is now," Amy muttered, looking away.

The girls walked on without saying anything more. The only sounds were the birds in the trees and the soft *plonk-plonk* of tennis balls on the lumpy school courts. A car squealed around the corner and roared past them, filled with laughing seniors who were about to graduate.

Amy sighed again. She was thinking that she had another two years at Seaview, two years of people remembering what she had done to Ernie at the dance, how she had embarrassed herself, two years of people secretly thinking about that every time they saw her.

She suddenly realized that Regina had been talking to her, and she hadn't heard a word of it. "What?" she asked, tossing her head, trying to force herself not to daydream, not to think.

"I said where were you last night?" Regina repeated. "I tried to call you, but you weren't home. Were you at Colin's?"

"Uh—no," Amy answered reluctantly.

They walked on for a while, turning the corner at the back of the football stadium.

"Well?" Regina asked. "Where were you?"

"Ernie's," Amy told her in a whisper.

Regina's olive eyes grew wide and her mouth

formed an *O* of surprise. "You went over to Ernie's house?"

"Just to see what he was doing," Amy said sheepishly.

"What?"

"Well, he didn't come over for dinner yesterday, so, I thought maybe I'd just stop by. You know, just for a second, and see how he was doing."

"And how was he doing?" Regina asked, rolling her eyes.

"Fine," Amy said, trying hard to sound casual. "Ingrid was over there. They were studying for finals or something."

"So what did you do?"

"Well, I guess I kind of stayed for a while and studied with them." Amy's normally creamy white face was a vibrant pink. She was looking in every direction except toward Regina.

"Wait a minute," Regina said, stopping at the corner, trying to remember something. "Didn't you tell me you went over to Ernie's house the night before?"

"Well—yes," Amy admitted. "But that was just because the twins had made something for him, and I was just delivering it for them. They made the cutest picture for him. I knew he'd want to see it, so I took it over."

"I see," Regina said. She put a lot of meaning into those two words.

"I was just delivering a picture," Amy said very defensively.

"I see," Regina repeated.

"I think we can change the subject now," Amy said.

"Well, what about Colin?" Regina had to continue the line of questioning, partly because she was curious, partly because she was enjoying seeing Amy squirm like this.

"What about him?" Amy asked irritably.

"Have you seen him?"

There was a long silence. "Well, no," Amy said finally.

"You mean you—"

"I don't think I'll be seeing him," Amy said without emotion. "Actually, he told me he doesn't want to see me anymore."

"What?"

"Because of the dance. He said I'm a violent person, and he doesn't believe in violence. He said I'm too temperamental for him. He doesn't believe in temperamental either."

"Aw, I'm really sorry, Amy," Regina said with sincerity. "I didn't know—"

"It's okay." Amy shrugged. "No big deal. Really. I never liked him that much. I think I liked his car more than I liked him. In fact, I'm sure of it."

"So you went over to Ernie's house twice, and—"

"Let's change the subject now, Regina," Amy insisted.

"No, I don't think we can."

"What do you mean?"

"Well, there go Ernie and Ingrid now."

"What?" Amy exclaimed, her voice rising to a pitch where only dogs could hear it.

Then she spotted them. They were holding hands and walking across the football practice field.

"'Catch you later, Regina!'" Amy cried and took off after them.

"Hey, wait up! Wait up!" Amy shouted.

Ernie and Ingrid turned around and saw her running at full speed toward them. Ingrid groaned and made two fists. Amy didn't notice. She did notice that Ernie grinned at her.

"Where are you off to?" Amy asked them, out of breath from her mad dash.

"Just going to get some pizza," Ernie told her.

"Great idea!" Amy exclaimed. She stepped between them, and draped one arm around Ingrid's shoulders, one arm around Ernie's. "Come on—let's go. I'm starving!"

"Okay!" Ernie said enthusiastically. He clicked his teeth.

That's so *adorable* how he does that! Amy thought.

The three of them walked across the field toward Pete's Pizza Heaven at the mall.

"Maybe we could study together later," Amy suggested. "I've got really good history notes. Chemistry too. I'll bring them over to your house after dinner, Ernie. Okay?"

Amy couldn't see Ingrid's face. But she could see Ernie's. He was giving her a warm and happy grin, that wonderful, lovable, fabulous grin that only Ernie could grin.

About the Author

"Where do you get your ideas?"

That's the question that R. L. Stine is asked most often. "I don't know where my ideas come from," he says. "But I do know that I have a lot more scary stories in my mind that I can't wait to write."

So far, he has written over a hundred mysteries and thrillers for young people, all of them bestsellers.

Bob grew up in Columbus, Ohio. Today he lives in an apartment near Central Park in New York City with his wife, Jane, and son, Matt.

Now your younger brothers or sisters
can take a walk down Fear Street....

R·L·STINE'S
GHOSTS OF FEAR STREET ®

1 Hide and Shriek	52941-2	/$3.99
2 Who's Been Sleeping in My Grave?	52942-0	/$3.99
3 Attack of the Aqua Apes	52943-9	/$3.99
4 Nightmare in 3-D	52944-7	/$3.99
5 Stay Away From the Tree House	52945-5	/$3.99
6 Eye of the Fortuneteller	52946-3	/$3.99
7 Fright Knight	52947-1	/$3.99
8 The Ooze	52948-X	/$3.99
9 Revenge of the Shadow People	52949-8	/$3.99
10 The Bugman Lives	52950-1	/$3.99
11 The Boy Who Ate Fear Street	00183-3	/$3.99
12 Night of the Werecat	00184-1	/$3.99
13 How to be a Vampire	00185-X	/$3.99
14 Body Switchers from Outer Space	00186-8	/$3.99
15 Fright Christmas	00187-6	/$3.99
16 Don't Ever get Sick at Granny's	00188-4	/$3.99

A MINSTREL BOOK